The Goalie

OTHER TITLES BY JIM CRUMLEY INCLUDE:

Scottish Landscape:
Something Out There
A High and Lonely Place
Among Islands
Among Mountains
Gulfs of Blue Air (A Highland Journey)
The Heart of Skye
The Heart of Mull
The Heart of the Cairngorms
St Kilda*
Glencoe – Monarch of Glens*
Shetland – Land of the Ocean*
West Highland Landscape*

Scottish Wildlife:
Waters of the Wild Swan
Badgers on the Highland Edge
The Company of Swans

Autobiography:
The Road and the Miles (A Homage to Dundee)

Fiction:
The Mountain of Light

*Collaboration with photographer Colin Baxter

The Goalie

Jim Crumley

Whittles Publishing

Published by
Whittles Publishing Limited,
Roseleigh House,
Latheronwheel,
Caithness, KW5 6DW,
Scotland, UK
www.whittlespublishing.com

Typeset by
Samantha Barden

ISBN 1-904445-11-X

Printed by
Scotprint, Haddington

REMEMBER WELL

Robert Walker Crumley
1875 – 1949

Peter G. Cavanagh
1930 – 2003

—Foreword—

The Goalie is written from the heart, and with pure tenderness and affection. I read it on a train journey back to my native Dundee where the book is set. As I crossed the majestic Tay, over the mighty rail bridge loved by all Dundonians, my eyes filled to the brim.

It is a book evocative of hard times, and of a proud city whose people have weathered those times with strength, courage and humour.

My own late father was a big Dundee fan and I was reared on tales of Billy Steele, Charlie Cooke and Alan Gilzean to name but a few of the Dark Blue legends. However, when a nip or two had been taken, he would recite at the drop of a hat the names of the men who brought the Scottish cup to Dens for the only time: Bob Crumley's name was first from his lips as the "Goalie", so for me this book has a particularly strong emotional resonance.

Jim Crumley has captured the spirit and the essence of what football meant, and still means to those of us in the city who love the game and its heroes to our very souls.

Jim Spence
Television and Radio Sports Broadcaster

—Authors Note—

Robert Walker Crumley was my grandfather. Some of the bones of this story are also the bones of his life. But so much of his life was kept from me that this is a fictional account of best guesses and some imaginings, a story based on a life. I know two things for sure: that he lived a better life than I was led to believe by his own family, and that on an April day in 1910, Dundee Football Club won the Scottish Cup for the only time in their history and sealed his fate forever.

A word on language, for the benefit of those unfamiliar with the nuances of the "English" language as practised in the city of Dundee. Dundee still has a vigorous Scots tongue in its head and uses it instinctively. Its estuary-wide vowels are its most conspicuous feature. For example, the first person pronoun "I" and anything that rhymes with it is pronounced "Eh", as in wet, but with a certain roughening in the throat. More famously, "pie" is "peh" and has become a Dundee cliché.

There is also a local vocabulary, some of it a remnant of old Scots, some of it unique. I have chosen to leave these words unexplained in the text, to be negotiated like sandbanks in the Tay estuary. If you get stuck, don't worry. You'll float off again soon. But this mini-glossary may help:

Breenge – barge in
Doup – polite form of arse
Een – eyes

Howff – a meeting place, usually a pub, and in this case, not to be confused with a Dundee graveyard of the same name.

Mellie – a rumpus, usually involving fisticuffs, often in a howff

Pavey – pavement (a Dundee characteristic, shortening a word then adding a –y syllable)

Pech – puff and pant

Stour (pronounced stoor) – dust, dirt, muck, air pollution

Stushie – commotion, noise in general

Whu' a fleg! – what a fright!

—Acknowledgements—

The author would like to thank the Scottish Arts Council for a bursary that greatly assisted the cause of this book.

Skylark, written by Hoagy Carmichael and Johnny Mercer, is published by Chappell Music Ltd

– 1 –

The trouble with family albums is what they leave out. What I mean is…family album faces are self-selecting. Only loved ones, no unloved ones, no black sheep. The son who resents having the sins of the father visited on him so relentlessly (will he never be free of the memory of that old dead haunter of his footsteps?) is going to compile a father-free family album. He cannot deny his father but his family album can.

So who's missing from this one? You know who I mean, eh? You heard the stories. And because you loved the faces who told you the stories, you swallowed them whole. Why wouldn't you? You were only a child. So was I when I first heard them, the same stories and I swallowed them whole. But ever since I grew old enough to think about them for myself, ever since I stumbled unwittingly over the first lie, I began to find that the pieces of the stories don't fit. I have found, too, that there are other pieces, pieces the stories deny or omit.

There is no place in the family album as you and I know it for the missing face. So I have started a new one, and I would like you to look at it, soon but not yet. Because before you look at its collection of photographs (it's not an extensive collection, it won't detain you long) I want to take you page by page through the photographs that are not there, the ones I could not find and the ones that were never taken.

Pour us a drink. Pull up a chair. Indulge your father this once.

-2-

Do you see the old blind man across the street, sitting alone on a low windowsill with his feet on the pavement, slightly bent at the waist, stiff as a rusted hinge? That's him. The Goalie.

They made a cigarette card of him, you know. The usual thing. Arms folded across his chest, a high-necked sweater which was all that used to distinguish a goalkeeper from the rest of the team in his day. Even in that wee portrait you get the sense of a tall man. Tall, slim, strong.

The face is handsome. Good jaw, bad moustache, although judging from team photographs from around the same time, the moustache came and went. Fair hair neatly parted and combed, wavy and slicked down. The expression is distant, wishing the camera wasn't there. I wish I could see the eyes better, know their colour. They took them out, you know. His eyes. They used to do that then when you went blind.

Anyway, by the time that cigarette card came into my hands it was eighty years old and he had been dead for forty. And it was black and white. So I'd still have to guess at the eyes. My guess would be blue, deep blue, like my own. Like yours.

There he is. The Goalie, an icon of his own streets, in his day.

Do you see what he's doing now?

Look how only his head moves. He's watching the bairns playing football in the street with his blind man's ears. He can do that. He went blind gradually and his ears became his eyes. See! He knows every move and who makes it. Their voices and their other sounds have become their faces. Do you see how he turns his head away from where the ball is? Turns an ear towards it? Hear how the noise always accompanies the ball.

Now, look over there, back across the street. See the young couple with the pram? Good looking couple. The man is pointing out the Goalie, saying something to his wife. Listen.

"There's Bob Crumley," he says. That's all. Why would he say that? Why would he not cross the street, clap the Goalie's shoulder and push his wife forward for the young woman and the old man to greet each other? But he never did. The two of them never met. He never introduced his own wife to his own father.

At the very least, why does he not say to her as he points:

"There's my father."

And do you see the bairn in the pram, a wee laddie, eight or nine months old? It's me! And the old man, the

Goalie, the man I'm looking at with a bairn's unquestioning, uncompromising stare, is my grandfather. And I was never introduced to him either.

He's famous.

Famous from one end of Dundee to the other for one April day in 1910 when he stood firm and Dundee won the Scottish Cup for the one and only time. Almost a hundred years later, it's still the only time. A hundred years of trying and still only that one heroic exploit. They say Dundee was drunk for a week, men handing round bottles of whisky in the street, day and night, to anyone who would pause long enough to drink.

He'll soon be dead.

He'll die not knowing I exist. That cannot be right, can it? Nor can it be right that he'll carry his son's grudge to the grave. And he has not graced his family album.

But I would like you to remember this picture of him, sitting alone on a stone windowsill at the top of a long, climbing street walled in by four-storey tenements built in stone the colour of mud, and listening to a bunch of bairns he cannot see, "playin' fu'bah" if you were to ask them what they were doing.

His whole life is there in what you see. Its beginning is the bairns in the street chasing a hard wee black rubber ball, "a sponger" they'd call it. Its end is that windowsill seat. It will serve me better than any gravestone after he's dead, long after he's dead and my own questions have begun to let a little light in on his life.

Between the bairns and the windowsill seat there is the game itself, which he loves, and which he lived for more than he ever did for any one human being. Oh, there was Jean, whom he married and who bore his six bairns and died young in the Spanish flu epidemic at Christmas 1918. And then there's Jessie, up to a point. But neither of them really won his heart, for the game had that.

The only thing that comes close to the game in his affections is his place on the map, his city, his Dundee. Sea-smelling, mill-clattering, lum-reeking, sun-facing, mud-coloured stone maze of tenement-walled streets perched between its two hills and its mighty river…Dundee is his holy city. It's his Jerusalem, his Mecca, and for that matter his New York and his London and his Paris too. It's all the world he needed or ever desired. And now that he is almost dead, perhaps he has begun to re-shape it in his mind's eye into his heaven, his Valhalla, or his Tir Nan Og more like, where a sporting icon is forever young.

When he lost Jean he lost his six bairns too, for they were taken irretrievably beyond his reach. He was instantly alone and lonely forever. As you see him. He has what the game left him and he has his place on the map. And what you see is all there is.

He has lived distrustfully with the adulation for forty years. The Goalie: it used to be his job description. It has become his name. Even now, when he walks into the Railway Tavern touching the door jamb with his white stick to confirm his bearings, forty years after the event, someone will call out:

"Mak wey fur the Goalie!"

And he'll walk through that amiable enough fug of Woodbine and banter and beer, him and his stick, like Moses parting the Red Sea. They all fall back, mak wey, and he finds the seat no-one else ever sits in. The icon's chair. There'll be a drink in front of him before he has sat down. They say he hasn't bought a drink in forty years, but maybe that's only because no-one else will let him.

But all he ever trusts is his loneliness, and the game did that to him too.

−3−

Look, the bairns' game's breaking up. Mothers are calling them in for their tea. The street goes quiet at this time of day. The shadow of the west side tenements climbs the wall on the other side, sunlight still colouring the top two storeys…well, colouring in the sense that the shade of gray-brown mud is deeper, a different shade of mud. You have to be born to that shade of stone to love it, and he was born to it, and he loves it, as individualistic a shade of stone as the folk who inhabit it. He's as hewn from it as any of them. But the game made him what he is, and in their eyes it made him different.

The Goalie's the only figure in the street now. He loves this hour. The bairns' voices have faded from his head. He's heard their feet on the stone stairs up the closes, heard the doors close at their backs (knows which voice belongs to which door), wishes he was one of them now, with it all to do again.

It's a love affair, you see. He loves the game, and for a while, the first half of his life, the game loves him back. The love between them only grows fiercer. Then, overnight, the game – fickle bitch! – turns its back, says "never again", beckons to a new goalie, younger of course, cheaper, but not fit to lace his boots. His heart breaks.

Time takes the game away from him, for the game is forever young. But he cannot stop loving it. He never learned that trick. And as you see, he still hasn't. The game left him its memories and forty years of adulation in the streets of his own city, and a hole in his heart like a mineshaft. No, worse than a mineshaft. A hole the size of the Lochee Tram Depot. There was never a bigger, blacker hole in the world than that.

Forty years he spends trying to come to terms with the hole. He knows by now that no-one, nothing, will ever fill it.

Oh yes, he's tried. He's trying now, alone in the street. But it's forty years man! Forty years, and he never learned the trick of it.

See how stiff he is when he moves. But see how straight he gets once he's on his feet, and once he gets going, how strong the stride, how confident the stick's rap against the mud-brown wall. This is what he will do now: he'll go to the corner where the sun pours in and the tenements on the far side blunt the east wind. There's another windowsill there where he can sit for half an hour with his feet on the pavement and warm himself against the cold black hole inside him. The city is content to let him be for a while in the empty sunlit street, alone with what he can trust, the very emptiness of the street itself. He'll sit again in the bright, echoing stony calm, a silhouette with a shadow three times his own length. The shadow sprawls far out across the street where he lives.

He tilts his head at the sun. His eyeless face still winces at the glare, as if there were eyes to be troubled by it. Do you know what he thinks, what he sees in his mind's eye? He's feeling how high the sun is in the sky, and guessing the dimensions of his long shadow, laying it out on the street. He thinks:

"Eh could've done fine wi airms and legs that lang when Eh was atween the posts!"

His mind's eye softens and smiles at him.

Then he sees a high, swirling ball coming in from the right, teased by the sea wind that forever cruises across Dens Park, that smooth green acreage that was his theatre, his stage, the green walled in by the massed faces of his own people. They would hold their breath in their thousands as he tensed under such a ball, waiting, waiting, timing, timing, timing. He could read that wind then like words on a page, and with a rare fluency.

He could leap into that wind early or late according to how he read it. When he leaped he rode that wind.

He always kept a slight bend in his lanky arms, so that he could persuade his legs to spring higher than they needed to. He cut the wind with the long edges of his hands, huge hands, hands built for the job. He could catch the ball one-handed if need be, but "two hands on the ball" was the solitary commandment by which he lived. "Two hands on the ball" fulfilled all his life's purpose.

So he curves his wrists in the last half-second of the ball's flight before the catch. The curve is crucial. With the curve in his arms and the curve in his wrists he achieves a cushioning and that brings control. If a goalkeeper achieves control, there is nothing anyone on the pitch can do about it, until he decides to let the ball free again. He loves that control. So he leaps higher than he needs to and catches the ball in his crucial, controlling curve. Crucial. He spoke the word to himself constantly, to remind himself to leap higher than he needed, and to leap with the curve.

And as he hits the turf again, he listens.

The response is as reliable as his own hands. His mind's eye is suddenly smiling. He hears it again now. The opened throats and exhaled breath of the gray-capped legions, then the encircling applause that runs fast around the terraces like fire before a dry wind. A roaring wind. He warms himself again before that fire in the empty street.

He stands tall then with the ball gathered against his chest, acknowledges with a grin the grudging back-pat of the thwarted centre-forward. Thwarting centre forwards is his life's work. He stands briefly at one end of a lush green oasis encircled by the gray reef of cheering faces in a sea of mud-brown stone, smiling and forever young.

And soon he will be dead. Old, stiff, blind, alone, dead, and by with it, free finally from the black hole.

—4—

The street drowses. No footfall, no horse-clop, no car. Cars haven't thickened the streets yet, not this far out from the city centre at least. Occasionally a muffled voice pierces the tenement walls, a careless spillage of family life out into the air of the street. It reaches the Goalie where he sits, the way an autumn leaf might let go and fall on a still November day. It's not November, though, it's April. The Goalie marks each dropped shout or laugh or bairn-screech, borrows them for a while, lets them punctuate his alone-ness. The things you hear by being still and listening when the rest of the world's just being itself.

He catches smells too. He's good at smells, better since the blindness of course, or at least more noticing. He puts smells to sounds, and with these his mind's eye makes pictures of the street, paints in surprising detail, makes poems of the workaday. He likes this one:

Eh'm blind. The wind
Up the street's ah smells
Eh never bathered wi
When Eh had een.

Bacon frehin's easy
(Even fur a lad *wi* een)
But the muhlk horse
Fae the coalie's is a wheen

O differences Eh never seen.
The day the Coalie cheenged
'es horse, 'e says, "Mornin Goalie".
"Eh like your new horse, Coalie,"

Says Eh. " He smells mair…licoricey
Nur the ahld ane.
And 'es coat's mair suhlky
Nur the Muhlkie's."

−5−

Shall I tell you what he has to do tomorrow? Today is April the 19th, 1950, so tomorrow is the 20th. Forty years to the day. Dundee 2 Clyde 1, after two replays. The Goalie is the last of that team alive.

He has a letter in his pocket, which is rare. He does not get many letters. When one arrives it troubles him because he must ask a neighbour, or Mrs Scrymegeour the home help to read it to him. Then he must ask whoever reads it to keep the knowledge secret, and mostly that doesn't happen. In the case of the letter in his pocket, it didn't happen again.

The Railway Tavern the other night, his stick on the door jamb, a voice from within:

"Mak wey fur the Goalie, star of stage and screen, Lochee's answer to Humphy Bogfart." The bar laughs and breaks into a spontaneous rendition of *As Time Goes By*, without words, like in the film… "Da-da da-da da-da, da-da da-da da-da…"

He waves his hand at them, as if he *is* famous. He is, of course, but not *that* famous, not beyond the streets of Lochee.

Lochee, where he was born and raised and lived and would soon die, a coarse-grained, self-contained outlier of Dundee, long since consumed by the growing city, but still, and always, itself.

He sits down, a hand on his shoulder, a tumbler of whisky set against the back of his hand. The gold meniscus rocks in the gaslit room and flickers with an echo of the fire at the far wall. He moves his hand to enclose the glass, softly, curving the wrist as he does so. Old habits. Sometimes he waits for the voice to identify his benefactor of the moment. Mostly he knows from the hand on the shoulder, the smell of the jacket, the footfall on the wooden floor. This time the smell is female. Jessie. Jessie Flight, wife of Wullie. They run the place between them. A kiss on the cheek like the brush of a fallen petal.

"Here you are Bob."

She's the only person in the whole of Dundee who calls him Bob any more, and even then only when she's close enough for no-one else to hear. To the rest of the city he's The Goalie, their property, a perambulating civic archive, old glories made flesh. But that "Bob" from the lips of Jessie is as sweet as the kiss.

"Cheers Jess."

"Eh hear you're to be famous all over again. Good for you. Eh should've married you when you asked me. Could've basked in your reflectit glory all these years."

"You made the wise choice, lass, as you ken fine."

She looks over her shoulder to where her man runs the bar, orchestrating its parliament of leaning cronies with an easy charm. She's ten years younger than the Goalie, and Wullie is ten younger than her. He keeps her young. The

Goalie keeps her wondering…what would it have been like? And what would it be like now?

Now he's old and blind and done in, and Wullie's handsomely middle-aged and easy to live with. The Goalie was married to the game. Marrying him when he'd asked her, thirty years ago, would have been a kind of bigamy.

"Maybe, Bob, maybe. Beer with that?"

She nods at his upheld palm-out hand that rebuffs the idea of beer as gracefully as it had once snatched sea-wind crosses from centre-forwards' heads. Even his no-thank-yous hark back to old glories.

The light touch on his shoulder lifting off, brushing his cheek where it had been kissed, her shoes on the wooden floor, the scent and the touch of her in the Goalie's mind, lingering then through the evening, a thread between them. In the minds of both of them, in the lulls that punctuate the hours of work and careless blethers, they wonder, even though it is all no longer worth wondering about. He never cared much for ideas that began with "if only".

A different voice, one from the body of the bar, a masculine corpus. It's too loud for anyone's comfort other than the ever-so-slightly-drunken owner of the voice:

"Show us the letter, Goalie!"

"Letter?"

Faked coyness, theatrical shrugs, playing the crowd again.

"The one invitin you to a posh soiree at the Palace Theatre, and ye've tae totter ower the stage, say a few words aboo' winnin the cup forty year ago an' tak a bow."

"Oh, that ane."

You see why he trusts only the shadow on the evening street?

–6–

He taps on Mrs Soutar's door across the landing.

"Agnes, there's a letter here Eh canna mak head nur tail o', except that it smells posh."

"Posh?!"

Her day's made.

"Okay, let's hae a look. Bring it in to the windie where Eh can read it for you."

So they stand side by side in the window and she reads him the tidings. Guest of honour. Dinner at the Queen's Hotel, variety show at the Palace…but in his head he hasn't got past the first bit. Guest of honour. The Lord Provost's guest of honour. Forty years after the event. The last one of the eleven alive. Not a moment too soon, eh?

"Thanks Agnes."

He turns for his own door, but he turns again, through the close, out into the street, taps down to Alex Smellie's shop with the look of the words "Guest of honour" in his mind's eye, the look of the words as he remembers them. They impress him, and now he wants to be sure of something. Alex Smellie'll ken. Alex knows words, does crosswords. In the shop:

"Yur early the day, Goalie. Whu'll it be?"

"Half loaf, Eck. Fehv Woobine."

The shop mercifully quiet…

"…And a wee favour, Eck."

"Favour? Of course."

"Have you got a dictionary?"

"Dictionary?"

"Are you gong to repeat everything Eh say?"

"A dictionary, aye, fur the crosswords, under the counter, but ye canna buy it…"

The Goalie sighs. Didn't think it would be this hard. He tries again.

"The favour is…could you just tell me what it says for 'honour', please."

"Honour?"

"Yur daen it again, Eck."

"Sorry, Goalie, it's just no quite your usual run-o-the-mill Monday mornin stuff…Look, ye dinnae need a dictionary fur that, it means…"

"Eh ken fine whu' it means, Eck. But Eh want the, em, the official version, the actual words. It's a good dictionary, eh?"

"Oxford."

Means nothing to the Goalie, but he beams his approval.

"Ah, an Oxford. Right, on ye go…"

So Alex Smellie licks his thumb, pushes through the pages, points an index finger, reads:

"Honour. Respect, esteem, reverence; reputation, glory, distinction; mark of distin…"

"Hud on, hud on, Eh've tae memorise this."

"Memorise…shit, sorry, daen it again. Whu's this ah about?"

"Patience, lad, patience. Now, after reputation…"

"Suit yerself. Glory, then distinction, a mark or token of distinction, high rank, nobleness of mind…"

"Whoa, whoa, Eck, that'll dae. Thanks. Eh'll see you later."

And Alex Smellie follows him to the door, stands there, scratching his head like a character in a *Sunday Post* cartoon, watches the Goalie tap his way back up the street, wondering: "Whu's got intul 'es heid?"

What's got into his head is the words. It was better than he thought. He looks at them with his mind's eye as he walks, taps his stick against the wall for every syllable. Re-spect. Tap tap. Es-teem. Tap tap. Rev-er-ence. Tap tap tap. He speaks the first six words aloud, with a natural rhythm, as if it was a football team line-up, starting, of course, with the Goalie.

"Respect, Esteem and Reverence; Reputation, Glory and Distinction…"

He laughs out loud:

"No a bad half-back line!"

"That you talkin to yersel, Goalie? Eh could get you locked up for that."

Double Eckie crunched across the street in his size elevens. Police Constable Alexander Alexander was the law in Lochee, where they were inclined to say to strangers that Dundee named the Law Hill after him. The Law is Dundee's flat-topped volcanic hangover and centrepiece. All the natives pech up there from time to time (the rich ones drive up its corkscrew road) for the view above the stoor, and for the air which is salt or sweet depending on the wind that blows it up from the sea or down from the glens.

And PC Alexander Alexander was Double Eckie to that portion of the world that crossed his path.

The Goalie knows the footfall as well as the voice drifting down from above him. Not many people's voices did that, but Double Eckie was double the size of most people too. The voice smites the Goalie's ear like a winter easterly on the top of the Law Hill, which is to say something both rough-tongued and reassuring, icy and warm, hard-edged and soft-centred as a sherbert lemon.

They were two big men and they liked each other. When they shook hands at New Year if was as if two shunting engines had coupled, the better to convoy some preposterous cargo to an inevitable destination. The Goalie's face rises towards the source of the sound and grins.

"Rehearsing meh lines," he says. "Eh've got a speech to prepare."

"So Eh hear. Just met Aggie the blah-baggie."

"So soon, eh? Thought Eh might at least have got the mornin tae masel, but God knows why."

Double Eckie grimaces in sympathy, takes his leave, the retreating tremor of nailed boots shivering the stone street. The Goalie turns uphill again, taps back up the street, the Guest of Honour choosing his words, picking his team, working out his tactics, then, as a cloud crosses his mind's eye, having second thoughts:

"If Eh decide to accept the invitation, that is."

Two hundred and seventy minutes of football forty years ago were responsible for this, thirty-nine years after he hung up his boots. It's all anyone remembers of his life. It's as if they have been waiting for this anniversary and decided to cash in their civic asset, reasonably confident he won't make the fiftieth one. Since the final whistle blew on the second replay and the Scottish Cup was coming back with them to Dundee, they had all died one by one, ten of that famed eleven, until he was all that remained.

He speaks another thought aloud:

"Death 10 Life 1."

He taps on back up the street.

Scent of coal fire and toast from an open crack of window, a snatch of *Music While You Work* on the wireless, a saxophone mercilessly flaying the middle eight of *Skylark*. He winces. That song deserves better, but he catches himself supplying the words as the sound fades behind him:

And in your lonely flight
Haven't you heard the music of the night?
Wonderful music,
Faint as a will-o-the-wisp,
Crazy as a loon,
Sad as a gipsy serenading the moon…

What words, he tells himself, what a song.

He loves skylarks. He has good reason to. In a way, it all began with a skylark. He loves that song too. No Hogmanay at the Railway Tavern could pass without his rendition, relishing the words, taking liberties with the slippery harmonies of the middle eight, just like Hoagy Carmichael used to do.

He could never see the point of Alex Smellie's crosswords, of stockpiling words under the counter like dirty books, or in your head so that you can play games with them. But to wrap words round Carmichael's tune like that, that was an angel's work. From the first time he had heard the song (Hoagy's own homespun account of his own song) he made it his business to find out the angel's name: Johnny Mercer. He revered that name, and because Hoagy Carmichael had written the music around which such words could live and breathe, he revered that name too.

His mind's eye watches the words for him. (He can still see the shape of the words, the way Beethoven could still hear the music in his head after his deafness had set in. In the Goalie's head, his sight is as good as anyone's – better, for it works in the dark.) With such a song at your command you can turn a woman's head or make a grown man cry, if he is the right kind of grown man. If the singer had known the right skylarks. He knows such a grown man, such a singer, used to see both when he looked in the mirror. The tears were not for the song but for the skylarks he had known.

And for the dream.

The dream was a part of him forever. He loathed it for what it made him remember, needed it because it memorialised all he had survived, all he had overcome, bitter-sweet, two-edged sword of a dream that it was. But the dream comes later.

–7–

The first skylark was this. He was seven, big for his age, barefoot and arse-less-breeked in the Lochee streets. There was a game of football, a mellie of fifteen-a-side bairns, the youngest six, the oldest maybe twelve. Nobody wanted to be a goalie in street football, so they took turns, reluctantly. The ball, when they had one, was hard and black and the size of a wee orange. Pudd'n Langlands belted it from five yards out. He was standing in the goal. Without thinking, he thrust out one lanky arm, and the ball stuck there in his hand. He looked at it, bewildered by what he had done. Pudd'n Langlands frowned. Then he put his fist between the Goalie's eyes.

Pudd'n Langlands was ten and fat. The Goalie was seven and skinny. It wasn't a contest. He ran. The blood from his nose spilled over his mouth, his chin, and blew back along his cheeks, dried there to war paint.

He ran through the streets. He ran away from the streets. He reached the end of a steep lane called the Cooie

Roadie, that being the way a crude species of edge-of-town farmer coaxed a straggle of cows to rough grazing on the slopes of the Balgay Hill, "the Hully" as he would call it. He took the Cooie Roadie up the Hully at the same flat-out gallop.

He stopped at the top, just before the trees, threw himself at the long grass, sobbed the wounded pride away, sat up at last, dried his eyes on his sleeve and looked about. The city curved away below him to the Tay. The river widened eastwards to the sea, a mile-wide miracle as it passed Dundee, wider than anything he could think of after it passed Broughty Ferry's wave-butting castle. He loved the river without thinking why. It was what made where he lived better than where anyone else lived, coming up the hill out of the streets until you could see the river. That and the Hully itself, his very own place on the map of the world.

The city dozed in its Sabbath. No mill-reek from the lums. You could see for miles, seaward miles, the most mysterious of all miles. In his left hand, he could still feel the sting where the ball had clung on to his curved palm, that palm that curved round it despite himself.

What did he do that for?

His hand felt like he'd got the belt at school, but after the pain had worn off, so it was just stingy and hot.

What did he do that for?

He asked himself the question again. Then he wondered what it must have looked like to the other lads. Brilliant? Brave? Daring? Stupid? Really, really stupid?

His nose was numb. He felt it, miserably, with his fingers. Then quite suddenly he felt elated by it all, excited by what he had done. They would be talking about him, right now, the other lads, about how he saved the shot. Nobody ever talked about him before. He looked around again, at the falling-away fields, at his spinning, downhill city, at the flat-topped shape of the Law where it rose above the Lochee Road. The Law always seemed so close from the down-there of the streets, but from the up-here of the Hully you could see how the city clung to the Law's slopes and slid easily downhill to the river, the silver-and-yellow-and-gray-and-blue seagoing river.

He did not know yet that what he had done that morning had already marked him out as different. He did not know yet that that first save, point-blank, from the boot of Pudd'n Langlands, had already shaped the course of his life. What would follow was as inevitable as the Tay's first emergence from a high mountain lochan a hundred miles from here, a mountain called Ben Lui he had never heard of, but the birthplace of a lifeblood. The silver thread it unfurled down its mountainside grew into the inevitability of the estuary, the sweetness of the source blended at last with the salt of the sea. His first save was the sweet source.

He stands. Slim as a rowan tree, a sapling, but a strong one, well rooted, pliable in the face of his life's storms.

Then he hears the skylark.

He sees it step from the grass a dozen yards away, step up just like that, onto the air; sit like that, on an invisibile landing on its own invisible stair, and already singing. It sings and sings as it climbs its airy stair. Its stair goes through its roof, and still it sings and still it climbs. Then it finds another landing and sits there again, rocking on its wings, and the notes of the song are warm snow that falls about the Goalie's head.

He squints up at it, but it sings in the eye of the sun and the notes of its song are glittering scraps of sunlight in the Goalie's eyes. He puts a hand to his forehead like a brim to shield his eyes, and it's that laddie the farmer stumbles across – the raised hand, the face smeared with dried blood and dried tears and freckles – so that he says:

"A help ma Christ, it's Geronimo."

Wee Boab Crumley jumps half the height of the skylark. "Whu' a fleg, mister!"

"Sorry son. Whu's the matter wi yer face?"

"Playin fu'bah."

"Fu'bah? Are you no supposed to play fu'bah wi yer fu'?"

"Na. Eh'm the Goalie."

Eh'm the Goalie.

He hears the words. He feels his mouth make them. But it is as if they had already been implanted in him. As if he was just something the words had to go through so that the message could be announced to the world. Like the way a song goes through a skylark. He isn't much to look at when he announces it to the world, but then a skylark isn't much to look at either.

"The Goalie, eh? And when you're no bein the goalie, you're sneakin aboo' meh ferm watchin skehlarks?"

"Skehlark. Is that the bird's name?"

"Skehlark," the farmer confirms. "The blithest thing Moses let oo' the ark."

"Was that no Noah?"

"Noah? Moses never let Noah oo' the ark."

The boy shrugs. Then he gasps. He sees the bird fold its wings, hears it thud softly into the grass.

"The skehlark's fell!"

He runs forward, shouting:

"It's deid." Then,

"It's no deid, mister, but it's hurted."

He points to where a skylark hirples through the grass, trailing a wing.

"No laddie. It's no deid, and it's no hurted. In fact, that's no the same bird."

So he explains: how the skylark controls its landing, how it creeps through the grass towards its nest so that laddies like him – or foxes or hawks or cats or dogs – don't see where the nest is; how the sitting bird slips off at a signal and starts to feign a broken wing to lure danger away from the nest, and when its far enough away from the nest, the broken-winged one is suddenly cured and flies again, makes a long roundabout circle back to the nest. He leads the boy forward, ten soft paces from the edge of the field, kneels, parts the grasses to show the nest, an oyster of left-overs with four blotchy pearls.

"Feel."

The laddie touches the eggs, gasps again, wonder on his bloodied, tear-stained, freckled face.

"Warm!"

"Right. So let's awa afore they get cahld. Wee skehlarks dinnae hatch out of cahld eggs."

At the edge of the field again:

"How do ye ken ah this, mister?"

"Easy fur a lad wi een. Now awa hame and get ah that clart aff yer face."

He runs home, back down into the warren of stone streets, but with his head full of skylarks. His father looks up, sees the bloodied face, grins.

"How was the fu-bah?"

"Won 12-7." A small lie. He hasn't a clue who won.

"Good lad. Wash that aff afore your mother sees you."

He stops at the scullery door.

"Faither…"

"Aye?"

"Eh'm the Goalie."

His father grins again.

"Fine by me."

The cold splash in the scullery, sunlight and Sunday through the window, the water a silver thread tall as larksong in a skywards column, life affirming stuff. The water cold, clean, sweet on his tongue. His father calls through:

"Pudd'n Langlands was here for you."

His heart freezes. Life-affirmation on hold.

"Seems there's a game against some other lad's gang. Pudd'n wants you for 'es goalie."

His heart melts. Life flows again, sings, lark-like.

Wonderful music, faint as a will-o-the-wisp, crazy as a loon.

−8−

Pudd'n Langlands was in at the beginning of it all, then. He was in at the end of it all too, when the Goalie eventually hung up his boots. And he was in at the glorious apex of it all, the final, Ibrox Stadium, Glasgow, April 9th, 1910, and 60,000 folk crammed in.

It was like playing inside a gray mist, the walls of gray faces were so thick and so high, like an east coast haar blotting out the world down to so many square yards, but a warm haar that roared. Clyde were 2-0 up at half-time, strolling it. Five minutes from the end, five minutes away from winning the Scottish Cup, it was the same score. The Dundee legions in the gray wall had had enough, were beginning to turn for the exits, feeling a long way from home.

Three minutes to go. The Goalie makes one more save, leaping upwards and outwards. Logic said punch it, for it was the very extremity of his reach and he was already flying. But it was past logic now. His left fingertips clawed past a climbing head, felt the ball, dug in. The voice he had trained in his head screamed at him: "Two hands on the ball."

His right hand was going the other way from the ball, though, streamlining the flight of the leap. But he had gone as far as he needed to go now, further than he thought he could ever reach. As the ball began to slither against his left palm, the right arced up and clamped it. He hit the ground and heard it again, the gray music, the grateful opened throats, the applause that ran round the ground like a fire before a wind. Wonderful music…

So he stands. The ball is in his arms, under control and he sees Sailor Hunter hoist an arm on the halfway line then start to run. The Goalie frees the ball, unleashes a lifeline, his longest, straightest, truest clearance. Only it's more than a clearance. It's the drop-kick he has practised since he was seven, and as it crosses the halfway line and begins to dip, it yields to the spin he has given it by kicking it slightly off-centre. It curves as it falls, curves into the feet of the sprinting Sailor Hunter. There is a collision with a Clyde defender. The ball ricochets twice, but Hunter refuses to stop running and the ball emerges in front of him, rolling towards an open goal. He simply keeps it company, escorts it across the line, picks it up before it touches the net, runs back to the centre spot with it, places it, runs to the edge of the circle, turns and waits for Clyde to kick off again. 2-1.

Thirty seconds left. The Goalie snaffles a deep cross from the left, sees Jimmy Bellamy on the right, throws it low and fast. Bellamy runs and runs. The gray legions roar at him, a hot wind at his back, wings at his heels. His cross is the most perfect event of the afternoon. The boot that meets the cross, meets it on the volley with a fat thud that falls on the Goalie's ears a hundred yards away as music, is the boot of Pudd'n Langlands. The last kick of the game. 2-2.

It took two replays to prise the cup away from Clyde. But when Pudd'n Langlands finally put music between the Goalie's ears instead of his fist, the Goalie knew Clyde's spirit was broken. However long it took before the deed was done, it was music that won the Scottish Cup and brought it home to Dundee. Wonderful music, crazy as a loon.

–9–

Do you know the Railway Tavern? It's a wee red sandstone pub underneath what's left of the old Lochee Station that's the Burns Club howff since the trains were shunted off the map. Let me show you something in the Railway Tavern, a Friday night, 1941, the street blacked out and tholing the war as best it can. It has to do with the second skylark and the dream. You remember I mentioned the dream?

In he walks. The usual shout:

"Mak wey fur the Goalie!"

He makes the cheerfully ritualised entrance, sits at the accustomed corner, and Jack Davie the stationmaster ("Jack o nae trades, master of one," as he was apt to bellow whenever the drink took him, acknowledgement in its way that Lochee Station never took much mastering at the best of times and this was not one of these)…Jack says to him:

"See you've made it through the black-out again, Goalie."

"Ah the same to me Jackie. Been blacked out mair nur ten year."

The whole bar laughs. They all love him. His every pronouncement is either funny or wise or somehow enviable. He's one of them and they love him for that. But he's different from them too, gone beyond them, been a hero, and they love him differently for that. Because he never left them. Because they think he needs them to get by. And in a way he does. And in another way that's as different as the two ways they love him, they're the last thing he needs. You see, what he needs is what was taken from him, what he can never have back.

His bairns? Yes, he would like fine to talk with one of his sons, to hug one of his daughters, to know they still think about him. But he's reconciled to that loss. His sight? Certainly that, to look out over his city to the river from the Hully, to squint up into the sun at a skylark, to see what time had made of his bairns, of Jess, but he can handle that darkness too.

But the game, that football life, that cameraderie, that physical wellbeing, that confidence, that fire, that throat-tightening fire that kept him awake late on a Friday night and sprung his step every Saturday morning. He could not remember now the last time his step had sprung, and whenever all that crossed his mind, which was often, it depressed him profoundly, and there was nobody who could ever begin to understand.

In their loving ways, in their caring, they feed him. They feed scraps of the game back to him, crumbs of comfort, mutton dressed as spam, poor fare to be sure, but fare enough to keep mind and body together for an hour or two at time.

So you see, in a way he needs them, and in another, he can never let them so much as glimpse the truth of his alone-ness, and that is all he trusts. He thinks perhaps he trusted Jean in his glorious years, but he knows that time has misted the married years, that the jealous game corrupted them and bewildered Jean, and he could never explain it.

He sits quietly for an hour, listening, watching the room with his ears, sorts out who's in and who's missing, tuning in to this conversation, tuning out of that one. In that frame of mind, that internal stillness, and with none of the eye's capacity for mischievous distraction, he knows more about the small events of the room at any one moment than anyone else in it. He likes the corner of the table, his back to the wall, the wall that faces the bar. From here he knows who's got something to say, who's chatting for the sake of it, who's havering, and who's talking pigshite.

At the next table there are strangers' voices mingled with the familiar, two lads on leave from the war, reliving Dunkirk for the benefit of whoever would buy them a round. Jackie has just obliged. He leans back in his seat, so that he can enveigle the Goalie into the conversation if he's willing. He talks over his left shoulder:

"You stuhll there, Goalie? Yur affie quiet the night."

"Eh'm just a quiet kind o lad, Jackie, Eh was that well brung up. Stuhll here though."

"Just thinkin," says Jackie, "listenin to the lads there aboo' Dunkirk…you were in the last ane, eh?"

"The last Dunkirk?"

"Wahr, Goalie, the last wahr."

"Eh was there, though it wasnae the last ane, was it? An' neither's this ane."

"Whu' d'ye mind o it, though? Now, when you think back?"

He heaves a sigh that would blow away the Law Hill if the pub wall wasn't in the way. The pub wall has heard it before and holds firm.

"*So* long ago," he says.

"Ye mind 1910 well enough," prompts Jackie, but the smile or the joke he expected back doesn't materialise. Instead:

"That was fu'bah Jackie, an' fu'bah's life. Wahr's got fuck-all to do wi' life."

A wee shunter thuds into a string of wagons up above and the sound snakes along the roof of the bar. His ear follows it. Then, a silence, so deep you could drown the Law Hill in it. Jackie regrets leaning back in his chair now. He rocks forward again, putting its two front legs back in contact with the wooden floor. The Goalie's voice leans him back again.

"Whu' Eh mind, Jackie, is…"

The silence again as he gathers himself, sitting straighter, silence as black as the outside night. The shunter shudders, going backwards above their heads, over the bridge towards Carnegie's sawmill, followed by wagon-squeal, the noise as much a part of the place to them all as their own conversation. The Goalie measures the weight of the rest of his sentence while Jackie's chair sways uncertainly on its two back legs. Is the old bugger going to mind something or not?

"…is a dream."

Three voices at the next table, sounded as one:

"*A dream!*"

"A dream. And skehlarks."

The Dunkirk lads had wanted more than this.

"Some fuckin wahr you had, ahld man. Maybe if ye'd opened yer bloody eyes, ahld man…"

The drink talking. And they are kicking away their chairs and up in search of a more enlightened ear to bend. They find their way to anywhere other than the door barred by Jessie's flame-haired five-feet-three.

"No-one talks to my friends that way. Not in here. And especially not to that friend."

"Some thanks we get for fighting to save you miserable bastards…"

But the Dunkirk voices are too loud, drunkenly incautious. They travel the room, and from the game by the fire there is first the sound of dominoes being laid down – carefully, face down – four hands of them. Then the scrape of four chairs. Then Doug Flett, the blacksmith, says in a voice as soft as gaslamps:

"Trouble here, Jessie?"

"They're still thinking about it Doug."

The Dunkirk lads weigh the odds. It has grown darker since the blacksmith stood. Some shadow. Two young ones against four who certainly couldn't catch them if it came to it…

Then six more glasses sound pointedly against table and bar counter. Six more men are on their feet. Two against ten. Jackie abstains, but it could just be two against eleven. Dunkirk was bad, but there were friendly boats offshore if you could get to them. Here there is only a blacked-out and friendless street and the overhead screech of the wee pug slamming into the solar plexus of a wagon. The wagon grunts, then squeals. The Dunkirk lads leave, going backwards, not straight.

"Thanks Doug, thanks boys," says Jessie.

She passes the Goalie's chair on her way back to the bar, pauses with her hand on his shoulder, says softly:

"You're right, Bob. War's got fuck-all to do with life. Let me fill that for you."

He touches the hand before it lifts off his shoulder, nods his thanks. In his head there is a skylark, singing flat out and high over France, and a dream that haunts.

– 10 –

He fended off the dream. He could do that, if he was awake, if it was the waking version of the dream. It could touch his waking and his sleeping darkness, but if he wanted to, if the will to resist it was on him, he could turn the waking dream back and watch it fade away, the way the Victoria Arch would get spirited away by the sea haar breathing in past the docks.

The Vicky Arch? Before your time, a brutal, free-standing monster at the entrance to the docks. Wee pugs like the Lochee station ones used to rumble underneath and blow smoke up its skirts, a nice two-fingered gesture if you think about it now, now that the Victorian legacy is seen for what it really was, now that the Vicky Arch is long gone.

Older generations had a different approach to it. The Goalie was born when Victoria was still around, remember, and saw the thing rise out of the stour. Dundee rarely built with taste in recent centuries, but it never lacked self-confidence. The arch was as self-confident in its way as Cox's lum, the first and last great totem of the jute years. They tried to knock it down a few years ago. The place nearly rioted. That's Dundee for you, a city in love with a lum. The Vicky Arch had none of its grace and style. It was just bloody big and bloody Victorian. Anyway, one day in the seeing half of his life, he's waiting for a bus at Shore Terrace, and the haar rolls in up river from the sea, dulling the noontide and shining the stone streets, and as the Goalie stands there, the stuff snaffles away the Vicky Arch before his very eyes. The eyes were maybe going by then, the right eye more or less gone since the end of the war to end wars, but he still sees enough that day and he's full of it when he gets to the Railway Tavern that night.

"It was the power o the thing. The wey you could see it comin, wipin oo' this landmark and that, spillin owre the banks o the river, and nothin anyone can do aboot it."

He shakes his head, marvelling.

"Nothin."

Then:

"Back in the wahr, when you saw them comin at you, you could aye fight back, knock holes in them. No this stuff. It was the speed it came in – no fest, no slow, no reasonin wi' it. Ye cannae knock holes in haar. Eh saw it comin across the docks and Eh thought: 'It's makin aff wi' the Vicky Arch!' And so it did!

"Eh got aff the bus at Logie Street so's Eh could awa up the Cooie Roadie an look doon on the stuff. The hale o the middle o the toon's awa, and the river wi' it."

He shakes his head again.

"Just gone. Just nothin. It was the power o it. Could just snuff oo' the Vicky Arch!"

He learned from that visible expression of irresistable power, and he invented his own. The haar showed him the way. It was tiring work, resisting the dream, and he grew less and less inclined with the years, but now and again he would summon his defences, dig in, hold his line, test his own resolve, perhaps just to see how much of him still lived. Two hands on the ball. That old precept.

How he fended off the dream, if the mood was on him, was this: he could throw something else into the forefront of his mind with all the force that vivid darkness could muster. He might, for example, imagine a turbulent, swirling sea wind at Dens Park, the high drop kick too unreliable. But he had a flat-armed technique for throwing the ball low and hard and fast and under the wind, the power and accuracy often startling his own player as he ran on and took the throw without having to break stride (if it was a perfect throw-out, the consummation of his trade, the apprenticeship dating back to that day when his seven-year-old self felt the full weight of Pudd'n Langlands's fist). That kind of throw could fend off the dream.

But he had to have something to throw, a force which the dream would have to reckon with. What he threw into the forefront of his mind with all his power was a face. Margaret.

He despised that face. Or perhaps he pitied it.

Perhaps, because of his long isolation, and the long enforced self-containment of the blindness, he saw little or no difference between pitying and despising. He watched that face smile, heard it laugh, and at the sound of that laugh he felt in the back of his throat the almond bitterness for all the years that had passed since he began to associate that face with that taste, for he was quite capable of reinventing it pure and new-minted, a fruit of his other darkness that had nothing to do with the blindness.

You know how you take a hyacinth out of the darkness and there is the new green, slim, pointed thrust of the thing that is the fruit of the dark incarceration? It was that kind of bitterness, with the same kind of pungent fruition. He could almost take it out of the darkness and marvel at it. These were the kind of new things a blind man might discover, things born in the darkness, as opposed to the old, remembered things. They are not all bitter, not by any means all of them, but they are things rooted in shades of darkness the rest of us have no knowledge of – inner places.

So why would the face of one woman nurture such bitterness in a man not easily given to bitterness? If you were able to ask him now, he might say, by way of introduction:

"Oh, but she was cahld."

Cahld.

He would pronounce the word two or three times more with long pauses filled with remembering, shake his head with every pronouncing, shrug at last, a "what can I tell you" shrug. What he could tell you if he had a mind to (but he probably wouldn't – he was loyal to his obsessions, whatever, but if he could…) might be…by way of introduction:

"Oh but she was cahld, son."

Then he would shrug that "what can I tell you" gesture. What he could tell you might be…

Aye, "might be", because there is no record of these things. But remember I told you about the bairn in the pram. How the Goalie never knew I existed? Remember my father pointing him out to my mother as if he was an untouchable celebrity? Don't you think that whatever was responsible for that distance between father and son might invoke bitterness in the father? Even a father not given to bitterness?

The truth is, of course that there is no way of knowing, not from the pages of a family album, not from the dead mouths of the family when even their living mouths were so confused and deceived. But I am trying to read his mind from what I have discovered for myself, from what I know to be true. I have been trying for a few years now, trying to decide honestly, in my own mind, what could have made sense of it all. I'm trying to explain to myself, to you, what my father and mother left unexplained, and what my mother made nonsense of after my father's death. She undoubtedly believed the little she told me, but it was nonsense for all that.

And the one thing that would make sense would be so unpalatable to my father and mother that I hesitate to spill it out, as if even the suggestion would somehow invite their outrage from beyond the grave. For it is that Margaret – in the Goalie's mind at least – was the villain of the piece. Margaret, the beloved spinster matriarch my father idolised and taught me to love in my unquestioning childish way. My father and his five brothers and sisters all revered her. It was a difficult conclusion to arrive at, yet the evidence of those photographs not in the family album, not taken, not kept if they were taken…all that is damning stuff.

So what he might tell you could be something like this:

"Oh but she was cahld, son.

"Cahld…cahld…cahld…."

Then the shrug. Then:

"Tall and comely in her way when Eh first met her, so's Eh turned my eye on her afore Eh ta'en up wi Jean. It was her laugh Eh fell for – it lit up her face and took your ear like a skehlark singin. That's what Eh fell for, the first few times…but, nah, unkind to skehlarks, son.

"There was none o that, that throb you gett aff a skehlark when it's really goin for it, none o that passion, that purity…aye that *pure* thing (it sounds like *joy* but Eh never learned whether a skehlark kens a thing aboo' joy, or whether it just does that because it's a skehlark and that's what skehlarks dae)…anyway, it's maybe just that pure thing of just bein alive.

"Margaret was cahld. Skehlarks are wahrm. She never knew what that felt like, that kind of wahrmth.

"Eh'll tell you a thing. Eh saw her, no fehv year ago. Didnae actually *see* her of course, no havin een, but met her in the street. The woman she's wi' says:

" 'That you, Goalie?' "

" 'Edna!', says Eh. Eh never forget a face, especially one that looks like a thorn bush in a big wind. Then Eh hears a shuffle beside her. 'That Margaret wi' ye?', says Eh.

" 'Aye. You're lookin well,' says Edna.

" 'Eh'm sure you are too,' says Eh, 'but Eh havnae a clue.'

"She laughed and Eh waited for Margaret's laugh, that laugh that first turned meh heid ah those years ago. But ah she gied oo' wi' was 'Sss, sss, sss' through a mooth that never opened. She'd grown that cahld she'd frozen her ain laugh into silence.

"Tell ye, son. Eh gie thanks tae a God Eh dinnae really believe in for *no* bein married on her these last fifty year. Eh did better for masel marryin Jean, for ah that we had nae mair than ten year thegither. Fur ah that she died, Christmas 1918."

– 11 –

Christmas Eve 1918. A field in France. Where in France? Who the hell knew. Not Lance Bombadier Robert Walker Crumley. Three years of looking at the inside of trenches and the blown off bits of other men and wondering when the next severed head would be his own had made a scarecrow of an athlete and sand of his brain.

Guns.

Mud.

Water.

Blood.

Pieces of people. Neither friend nor enemy then, just pieces, not attached.

Noise.

Noise such as he had never known, he who had scored his finest hour with the choired throats of 60,000 footsoldiers, the impassioned legions of his own mud-coloured streets.

Fear.

Fear that was white in the night and cold in the heat and hot when you shivered. Fear was the only wound he had sustained in three years. It had ripped a four-inch wide gash through his middle from his back to his belly, so that his below-the-waist moved independently of his above-the-waist. He had measured it once with his thumb and finger.

"What size is that, Alfie?" he asked the nearest face. He called all faces Alfie. This particular Alfie looked at the spread of his finger, said,

"Four inches. Why?"

"That's how wide meh wound is."

"Wound? You havenae got a wound. That's why we hang around you. You're lucky. You won the cup. You'll win the bloody war for us. We're going home with you. You're the lucky mascot for this whole shitty trench. There's no wound. You havenae got a wound. You're not going to get a wound. You're lucky, and because of that, we're lucky. But it's four inches."

The last gunfire of Christmas Eve put Alfie's head at the Goalie's feet. Then it stopped for Christmas.

A voice, accustomed to ordering:

"Crumley!"

A reflex response, like a penalty box save:

"Sir!"

"C.O.'s tent. At the double, soldier. You're out of here, you lucky bastard."

"Sir!"

–12–

The C.O.'s tent. What could it mean? He had no way of asking himself the question. His mind was in the mud looking at Alfie's broken head.

Lucky.

Two people had called him lucky. His brain was sand. There was nothing with which to ask the question, that one or any other. An order said C.O.'s-tent-on-the-double-soldier, and to the best of his ability, he carried it out, not that it was much of a double.

In the tent:

"At ease soldier. Cigarette."

Two commands. He at-eases, he takes the cigarette which the C.O. lights for him, drags on it. Thank you, Sir.

"No easy way to tell you this, Crumley. Not after what you've been through. It's your wife."

He pauses to consult the paper in his hand.

"Jane?"

"Yes Sir. I call her Jean, but Jane is her given name. Sir."

Jean? What had this to do with Jean? Jean, looking up from the pavement, blood on her knee. Blood, a wound, what wound? There is no wound. But it's four inches, said Alfie, just before his head was wrenched away.

The C.O. is speaking again:

"Spanish flu. An epidemic. She did not survive. She is dead, soldier. I'm so terribly sorry. Do you want to sit?

"No Sir. No thank you. Sir."

"You're a good soldier, Crumley, fought a good war. What did you do before?"

"Footballer, Sir. Professional. Sir."

"Ah. Too late now for that, perhaps. Still, you're young yet. Sorry your war ends this way. But you'll be in Scotland in time for New Year."

"Thank you Sir."

"Questions?"

"No. Sir."

A hand on his shoulder, the C.O.'s face briefly close to his.

"That right eye of yours all right?"

"Yes Sir. Thank you Sir."

Outside the tent:

His mouth moves. He tells himself what he has told himself every day since it began:

"Two hands on the ball, soldier."

-13-

Let's leave him for a minute, eh? Leave the poor, skeletal, uncomprehending, shell-shattered, brain-deadened wretch and his travel warrants back to Dundee from his end-of-the-war wherever in France. Leave him, the lucky bastard.

Here are two more snaps you won't find in the family album because they were never taken. One shows two country girls, up-country Angus, one full-figured and fair and 18, the other only 15 but already taller, dark, quick. Sisters, Jean and Margaret Anderson, Jean the quieter one, dreaming of bairns of her own and a good man, a house with a view of the sea, enough money for hats, then enough for her own hat shop; Margaret the dancer, the laugher, the head-turner, not given to dreams.

They were mill lassies. What lassie wasn't up the Lochee High Street, where Cox's gargantuan monolithic lum was the totem they bowed to, then they turned their faces to the looms?

Shifting, piecing, spinning,
Warp, weft and twine,
They fairly mak ye work
For yer ten and nine…

Remember that song? That was them. The photographs show only the profile of the lassies. They face the looms, thole that roar, that clatter, hours and hours of hideous din, six days out of seven, for shillings. Yet you find their like (grown old) today down at the Verdant Works that has turned a jute mill of all things into a tourist trapping, only you're more likely to find not tourists there but old biddies of eighty-something spinning yarns to each other about their youth in "the muhlls", rose-tinting away the awfulness, commemorating instead the friendships that lasted the lifetime of the first one to die, proud of what they did because it stamped their city's name on the map of the world again, just as the whalers had done. But this time it was a woman's world, a woman's workforce. It was women's backs the Cox brothers grew rich on, women who made the great lum reek, women like Jean and Margaret, arm-in-arm sisters from the country, living with the stushie and stour of that seething corner of the city, sending shillings home, looking for Prince Charming up a close and the key that would unlock the mill doors and set them free, forever.

Jean would die at 30 with six bairns aged between two and eleven in the same three-roomed tenement where her Prince Charming had first lured her. And when she died, Margaret took the bairns in and brought them up and put distance between them and their father, and when she died she was a spinster of 85.

But if the photographs *had* been taken, you'd have seen two profiles facing the loom, hair tied back and piled high (a woman caught by the hair in one of those mechanical jaws died a slow and hideous death), high-necked, floor-length working dresses gathered at the waist, buttoned at the cuff, long apron smothering the curves of their bodies to nothing more than suggestions. If they spoke at all, it was in yells, and there are those who say that Dundee learned its distinctive estuary-wide vowels from the lassies who worked the mills and opened their lungs to make themselves heard.

But here they are, two foot soldiers in that army of women, workers for the common day, lightening the load of ritual and din with jokes about their gaffers knowing they could never be overheard, and with the tranquility of daydreams. He is out there. He is. All life's possibilities are out there, waiting.

The city seethed with them. It was gray and close-quartered and stonily confiding in the curve and climb of gaslit streets, and airy and cool on the hills, and when you dared its docks or took the salted air of its waterfront, its seagoing instincts crashed into the streets and the world was its oyster. And sometimes it felt as if Dundee was the world's oyster too, so eager and teeming and far-horizoned was the traffic at its waterfront. A lass from Inverarity could not help but be excited by the place.

Its streets smelled of horses, the closes of people living too crammed in for comfort, and the whole place was never still and rarely quiet. Saturday nights, a kind of street-fighting justice perambulated, especially where the Irish immigrants sallied forth from their enclaves and mixed it drink for drink, insult for insult, punch for punch and song for song with the natives.

Lochee was a microcosm of all that, save that it was as far from the waterfront as the city allowed. Double Ecky bestrode its stone streets dispensing all the justice that might be needed beyond what was meted out up dark closes. He was like a lighthouse come ashore and made mobile when he moved through a crowd, and just as visible, and no-one who ever remembered him remembered him in anything but his uniform. His life from the moment he uncoiled from his kitchen alcove bed to the moment he climbed back in was to be the law in the streets of Lochee. No other life occurred to him. He could bang heads together if he deduced it was the correct punishment, and he would cuff a bairn's lug or slip him a penny. He knew a stranger's business before the stranger knew he knew, and he set the supreme example which all Lochee followed: he looked out for folk. When he died, there were two thousand people passed his graveside in one day and for once Lochee fell silent. They say his widow never received a bill for the burial.

The Misses Anderson had not been in Lochee two days before they and he were on first-name-terms and winking terms, and he knew their home village, and that their father was a stone quarrier, and in general, he had charmed an autobiography out of the pair of them without them realising a thing. For fifty years, from the age of 20 to 70, he wore his own grooves into the pavements of Lochee, and no mortal was ever more content with his lot, and no lot more content with its mortal.

And he could easily have taken the second photograph, for he watches from across the street one Saturday lunchtime in 1905 when Jean Anderson bumps into her Prince Charming for the first time, only Prince Charming flattens her on the pavement and turns delighted eyes on her sister.

–14–

Monday night is the quietest in the Railway Tavern. He taps in, hears the quiet. Then Jackie's voice:

"Mak wey fur…ach make yer ain wey, ye ahld bugger, there's naebody here onywey."

"And good evening to you, young Jackie," he greets the voice.

Jess from the fireside:

"Come to the fire, Goalie. There's just us and Dougie."

The fire. That's fourteen paces, straight through the middle of the room. He finds the middle by holding his stick in his outstretched left hand until it taps a bar stool. Then straight down the room. He hears Jess cross from the fire to the bar, pour a whisky, splash of water, then her hand on his shoulder eases him into the seat where she's been sitting. He feels the whisky warm his throat, his gullet, his belly. He breathes out theatrically.

"Aaahhh!"

Then he turns across the fireplace.

"How's Dougie?"

"Never better, Goalie. Yerself?"

"You see it all, lucky buggar."

He likes wee blind jokes. It keeps out the darkness.

Darkness.

He doesn't like that word. The thing about the blindness was never to let yourself treat it with defeated words. They sink you. The blindness is a sea. You must tread its calmest shallows. In the calmest shallows, the sea is beautiful and at its brightest. A minister told him that once. As a rule he had no time for ministers, but he liked that one. Some funeral or other.

"How would you know that?" the Goalie challenges this minister, "you wi yer twa good een."

The minister is grateful for the kind of conversation that rarely crops up at funerals.

"My father told me. He was at Loos."

"Ah, him too."

"You were there?"

"I was."

The Goalie and the minister nod sympathetic silences to each other, like small, formal bows.

"How is he, your father?" the Goalie asks him.

"He didn't last five years after the war. He seemed to die from the brain down, bit by bit. He couldn't take his own advice. It defeated him."

The Goalie puts his left hand on the minister's right arm. Then he holds his right hand out for the minister to shake, a tiny wet patch on the hand the minister offers back, where a finger brushed a moist eye.

The Goalie says:

"It is a privilege to be able to cry. You need eyes to do it. The calmest shallows – I'll look out for them."

The minister says:

"It's supposed to be my job to bring comfort to the suffering."

The Goalie answers:

"And mine to be a safe pair of hands. Anyway, who told you I was suffering?"

The darkness defeated him not once after that. He could remember the calmest shallows, what they looked like, how they felt. He remembered day trips to Carnoustie, the warm sand, the summer shore, the blue-green brightness, the colour of that sea, that endlessness of muted blue brightness that only the East Coast sea knows. Or Auchmithie up beyond Arbroath, the white surge at the mouth of the caves, puffins sitting out on the easy swell. The calmest shallows, remember. Brightness that belittles the darkness.

There was a time, of course, when the blindness was new, and he felt hard done by, too alone, too ensnared by darkness. But one way or another, life, and that minister, showed him there was perhaps light enough to get by. He had always wanted to meet that man again to tell him that. But he never even knew his name. It was not the sort of things you did, ask a minister his name at a funeral.

"Penny for them, Goalie."

Jackie's voice. The Goalie realises he slipped anchor minutes ago, drifted off downstream of the conversation. He comes about, noses into the shallows, the calm and bright reassurances of the folk at the table.

"I was remembering a minister."

"Jesus, you've got a good memory," says Dougie softly. "Wedding or funeral?"

The Goalie smiles, nods.

"Funeral."

"Ah. So it was memorable because…?"

"Because his father had gone blind at Loos, and couldn't handle the darkness. He died of the darkness."

"Can that happen?"

"I've heard of it. They can't cope."

"How do you cope, Goalie?" Jackie, putting both feet in.

"Jackie…!" Jessie's reproof.

"No it's okay, Jess. I'll tell you, Jackie. I had my bad days, until I met the minister. He told me about the sea, about the calmest shallows."

So he tells them what's been on his mind. Then he says:

"The thing is, it wasn't enough after a while. At first, it was good advice and I needed it, used it. But I was never much of a man for paddling in the shallows, and I began to need more."

"More what? Water?" Jackie, floundering.

"More courage, Jackie. *Then* more water."

"I will not creep along the coast, but hoist my sail out in mid-ocean under the stars…George Eliot." Dougie, full of surprises.

The Goalie nods his approval:

"Oh that's good. Eh like that."

"Don't follow," says Jackie.

"One of the lads up at Dens – you know we gather up under the stand, the blind lads? – he told me about Beethoven, how he could still compose after he had gone stone deaf, because he could still hear the music in his head.

He had learned the music when he *could* hear, so if he wrote down a G, he knew what it sounded like, even though he couldn't hear it. So if you were to say to me 'glass of whisky', I still know what it looks like even though I can't see it. And I can tell you that this one is near enough empty, even though I can't see it."

"That a hint?" asks Jessie.

"Not much of a hint, and not my best hint, but still a hint, aye."

And Jessie fills four glasses, pouring from the bottle. No-one counted much or measured much in such a bar on such a night. The Goalie's glass salutes her.

"The blindness is a sea," he says again, repeating the minister's words, "but you either settle for paddling in the calmest shallows, or…or you learn to swim so strongly that you can rely on the swimming entirely. Know that you can swim for your life when others wouldn't put to sea in ships.

"You see, Beethoven said much the same thing of his deafness, and it was at his deafest that he produced his most complicated and deepest music. Some people say it's the best music ever written, although they probably never heard o Hoagy Carmichael. Anyway these deaf pieces, what they call the late string quartets, are quite something. That's what ane o the lads up at Dens telt me."

"Must have been a right shite game if you were discussing Beethoven. And onywey, what kind o fu'bah fan goes to watch Dundee and ends up spoutin aboo' Beethoven?" Dougie's half-amused, half-intrigued murmur.

"Half-time chit-chat owre a peh, Dougie. And he was a surgeon. Until he went blind. You see, fu'bah and the blindness are much the same that wey: they don't care wha gets smitten by them.

"So when the surgeon laddie tells me aboo' Beethoven, Eh asked him if he had records or anything, the stuff he wrote when he was really deaf. He did, he said, and asked if Eh'd like to go and hear them. Eh would, Eh said, so Eh ta'en the tram to Ninewells, big hoose, lovely garden, and he played one of the 'late quartets'. When it was finished, he asked what I thought of it. 'Never heard anything like it in my life,' says Eh.

" 'That's funny,' he says, 'neither did Beethoven.'

"So Eh says to him, 'Right, swimmin it is. Eh've had enough paddlin in the calm shallows now.'

"And that, Jackie, to answer you question, is how Eh cope. But Eh needed the minister and his calm shallows as much as Eh needed the Beethoven bit later. And now, Eh can choose, depending on how Eh feel – shallows, or deliberately getting out of my depth, just to see if Eh can handle it."

"No feart o drownin then?"

"No Jackie. No feart o drownin."

"The blind leading the blind," says Dougie.

Jessie tips the bottle four ways and smiles:

"The blind leading the blind drunk."

So they while away the evening in quiet, companionable drinking, friends among friends who speak the same language, the whisky bottle dwindling like a candle, the drinkers savouring the one thing we got right in this country, once and forever and gave to the world. The Scot who never learns to be convivial in the company of whisky and one or two kinfolk or welcome strangers, never learns to feel it loosen and liberate the mind and bind evenings together…that Scot has let slip from his or her grasp one of the unique essentials of birthright. And so it was that with the door locked after closing time, and Double Ecky now in their midst to make sure all was on the right side of the law, the whisky tried to liberate the dream while the Goalie was still wide awake.

Jessie would never have asked him unless they were alone. Dougie would never have asked. Double Ecky only heard of the encounter with the Dunkirk lads second hand and had no appetite for an old man's dream anyway. But Jackie was a collector of other men's flowers. He, of all of them, revered the Goalie's celebrity, shone it the way he used to shine the brasswork up in the signal box before he became stationmaster and rose above such things. That first public mention of the dream had fired his curiosity. Here was treasure to hoard. He brought it up.

"Mind the Dunkirk laddies, Goalie?"

"Laddies, Jackie, just laddies. There was no harm done."

"No it wasn't that. It was…well, you said there was a dream. Eh was just wonderin. What sort o dream comes oo' a wahr like that?"

They all look at him. Three of them to see what he's going to say. Jessie to see how he's going to take the question. With the timing of the Old Steeple clock on the stroke of twelve at Hogmanay, a train thuds heavily overhead, buffering into the silence. Jackie, despite himself, pulls a pocket watch from his waistcoat. He knows which engine it is, what its number is, who the driver is, where the driver lives, who his wife is, how many bairns they have, what their names are, when their birthdays are, how much he gets paid, how much of what he gets paid goes on his rent, how much he drinks, and why he has a pinky on his left hand that's severed at the first joint. He grunts monosyllabic recognition of all that at the watch, returns the watch to the waistcoat, his eyes to the Goalie, raises his eyebrows to reinforce the unanswered question.

–15–

The Goalie marks the end of the silence with a nod and a sip.

"The dream kicks off with – you won't believe this – it's what they used to do. Go, on guess, guess what it was they used to use, the officers, the ones that sent you over the top. Two of them, always two of them. Guess what they used."

"A starting pistol."

"Nope."

"A rocket?"

"Nope."

"Ane o they flare things that hings in the skeh?"

"Nope."

"Megaphone."

"Nope."

"They got big dugs to run alang the trenches bitin yer arses?"

"Ha ha. Nope."

"Nae idea, then. What did they use?"

He has them now. He pauses. Timing. That old habit. He lets the pause drag. He imagines Jackie's furrowing forehead, waits for the exasperated intake of breath as Jackie prepares to burst the silence apart. Now.

"A whistle."

"A *whistle?!*"

"Just that. A bloody whistle."

"What...wi' a pea?"

"Eh?"

"Eh was just wonderin," says Jackie, "what kind o whistle, whether it had a pea or not."

"What difference does that make?"

"Ma'er o technical clarification, Goalie. Armed wi' that, Eh can hear the whistle, and in that way..."

"Oh Jackie, shut the fuck up. Sorry Jessie." Double Ecky, laying down the law, forgetting he was in mixed company.

The Goalie listens inside his head, then shakes it.

"Nae pea. A lang silver whistle, on a lanyard, no like a ref's whistle, and yet..."

Jackie interrupts again, wallowing in the detail:

"Twa officers, you said. Doesnae take twa officers tae blah a whistle. What did the other ane dae?"

The Goalie lightly clenches a fist, slightly raises and curves its index finger, a finger on a trigger, leans it over towards Jackie's temple.

"Marksman. Pistol marksman"

Two voices simultaneously:

"What fur?" Jackie, mystefied.

"Jesus sufferin Christ." Dougie, not mystified.

Jessie bites into the bottom of a finger, shakes her head.

Double Ecky stares at the darkening fire.

Jackie looks round at them all, catches up with them then, incredulous.

"So the pistol officer shoots you if you don't go over the top when the whistle officer blahs?"

The Goalie's nod confirms the unspeakable.

"Executed."

"Did you ever see it happen?" Dougie's voice, soft even by his standards. But the Goalie snaps back at him:

"In the Black Watch? Never!"

Jessie's sigh is the unspoken exasperation of woman at the passion of man for his wars, his intolerable strutting inclination to lock horns, make borders, his insufferable love of regiment, his ancient willingness to go over the top at the shrill of a whistle. Even this blinded old man, tormented forever after the war to end wars had finished with him by the demons inside his head, still rises to salute his regiment. The Goalie acknowledges her sigh.

"Eh can hear you Jess. And Eh agree with you. Now. No then, though, no then. And probably no now either, if Eh was that age again.

"And Eh'll tell you somethin else. Eh was first over the top, and the fastest over thirty yards of no-man's-land. It was the fu'bah trainin. Short sprints, day after day for fifteen years."

"Is this…are we…Eh'm lost, Goalie. Is this the dream or the real war?" Jackie, floundering in the mud of northern France.

-16-

The dream, like the stone of the city that bore him, is the colour of mud. Its whistle is the only clean, pure, wholesome thing. No. Not true. There will be the skylark that finally conquers the war to end wars, but that comes later. To begin, the whistle is the one pure, clean, wholesome event in a long litany of squalor, a squalor the colour of mud. The whistle instils in him, in the small of his back, the urge to spring up the trench ladders and hit the top running. But the moment he springs, the very instant of the first uncoiling of his springing muscles, all is mud. The ladder is runged with mud. The rungs give way under his springing, willing feet. The ladder is unwilling. The dream is unwilling. Only the springing and the small of his back are willing.

So he tries to reach a lanky leg up for a higher rung. But that too is mud and gives way. He grabs the sides of the ladder, hauls on them, slides up, slides back. He rams his rifle bayonet into the trench wall and stands on his rifle. It holds. A rung not of mud. He claws over the top of the trench. He reaches back down for the rifle but his arms are not long enough. The officer with the pistol shakes his head, frees the rifle, hands it up.

"Sir." The Goalie acknowledges, and under his breath he mutters:

"Ex-fuckin-calibur."

He gets to his feet, turns to run at the enemy guns.

He remembers the training sessions at Dens. A vivid green stains the dream for a moment, then becomes green mud, then just mud again. A whistle – with a pea – he hears it! He hears it! – and he runs flat out for thirty yards. It is further than he ever needs to run flat out, but thirty yards becomes his unbeatable distance. No-one is faster. He wins beer money in bets. A goalie with that kind of speed can make 50-50 balls into 60-40 balls.

Run.

Attack as the best form of defence.

The dream lets him believe that glimmer of past, that single technicolour glimmer of green and firm ground and biting studs. Then it swallows him whole, spits him out again, headlong and knee-deep in mud.

Run?

Just to take a step, just to stand upright, swaying for balance, that is the dream's new challenge, while the whistle shrills and shrills like a bayonet in the ribs, a clean cold steel in the ribs. Fall now, and you have a reasonable chance of drowning. Drowning in mud, trampled by the man behind and the man behind him, the trampling men not knowing what they have stood on, far less who.

He fails to drown, wonders if his rifle will work when he pulls the trigger, if he pulls the trigger.

Then the dream tosses him a miracle, casts his feet onto a green square. Firm ground under his feet, so firm he dances. He lays down his rifle, takes off his belt, arranges them in a cross, sword-dances round them while in his head a piper plays *Bonnie Dundee.*

Dance.

He dances the green square down into the mud, deeper and deeper in, and still he dances, the rifle and the belt still crossed on the surface of the mud. The German soldiers watch and laugh and forget to shoot him. He dances right through enemy lines on his buried green square that only he knows is there. The dream tells him in a voice that is like a German speaking English not to worry, that as long as he feels the firm green square beneath the mud, as long as he can dance on the firm green, he will come to no harm. So at every summons of the whistle, he takes the mud in his stride, digs in every footfall until it feels the firm green beneath him. And every time he comes in range of the enemy guns he smiles at them, pointedly lays down his rifle and his belt in a cross, bows to them with hands on hips and dances past them, and the piper in his head plays *Bonnie Dundee.*

They wave at him. Not once do they fire, nor he at them. But he dances past and when he is behind them he snaps:

"Hande hoch!"

And ten or twenty bewildered soldiers drop their guns and let themselves be marched back across no-man's land at the point of his gun, back through the mud and the gunfire. For the dream is loud as well as mud-coloured. The noise is worse than the mud. It terrifies. It is why guns were invented after all, to kill and to terrify. In the dream they explode not on the land and all around him but in his head, between his ears. Bits fall from inside his head. Rockfalls of broken bits of skull, loose membrane, broken veins, scraps of brain, bits of eyes. They all break loose when the dream-guns explode inside his head, and pile up inside the landscape of his skull like so much scree. No gun ever wounds him, not from the outside.

So the green square of turf, which he knew was nothing more nor less than the floor of the pre-war theatre on which he danced his footballer's dreams and made them live…that took him through the dream-war. And in the real war to end wars, Alfie called him lucky and thought that as long as he and the others clung to the Goalie's shadow he would see them through the war to end wars too. But Alfie and all the other shadow-clingers knew nothing about the square of turf, and the mud and the guns got them. And when the Goalie left the war to end wars, he left it alone.

He came back from the war to end wars with the seed of the dream sown in him, and when the war to end wars ended for him not with victory or celebration or hero's homecoming but with the death of his wife at home, the seed of the dream rooted and tortured the inside of his head and made of it a no-man's land of mud and gunfire and other people's deaths and broken bodies, and these were his homecoming.

But the dream had left him, too, with a straw to clutch, one straw of hope with which to fend off the crushing weight of the guns, to assuage the grief of the world that warred on in his head. There had been one day during that real war to end wars that the guns fell suddenly silent in a purple spring dusk. That silence was so sudden and so startling that he learned then and there to love forever after the quiet of dusk, because in it, all sounds lived.

The wind's sigh lived.

The rain's weeping lived.

A footfall in mud lived.

Men who moaned at their wounds lived – as long as they moaned, they still lived.

Then he heard the thing which could cancel out even the war to end wars, and in time, would even defeat the dream. In that twilit calm in a field in France with the smell and the sight and the taste and the touch of the war to end wars corrupting four of his senses, he heard the song of the skylark.

His mind flew back. Back to Britain, to Scotland, to Dundee, to the Cooie Roadie, to the high slopes of the Hully, to the day Pudd'n Langlands bloodied his nose and he announced to the indifferent world:

"Eh'm the goalie."

The dream, even as it began to haunt him, adopted that skylark and gave it to him for a talisman, and over the years of the dream, the larksong grew stronger and stronger. He would feel himself willing it to be heard, a thin stream of…of pure…of just pure.

Behind the guns, under the percussive cacophany his head could not silence, he wove in the skylark, like Beethoven striving not to hear but to be heard. And always the dream would silence its own guns in the dream-dusk and always the skylark's uninterruptable song filled the void with the pure. And hope was reborn in him, and he awoke hearing not guns but larksong.

In that perverse way, the dream sustained him, kitted him out for survival when the war to end wars had done with him and left him alone on a train to Dundee between Christmas and New Year, the year of our Lord, nineteen hundred and eighteen.

–17–

Can you imagine that journey? Can you see him, sitting upright and unsleeping through the night, unthinking and unspeaking, unfeeling and uncomprehending. Then, after the long blackness of the winter night, the dawn, the sluggish sea-born dawn of the east coast, the pale illumination of the low-slung green world of Fife, and suddenly, as if he has just repossessed himself after some long vacancy of the spirit, he looks up and blinks because he is looking at something he can remember. He stands, hauls on the leather strap that lowers the carriage window. The sea air rushes in. He leans out into it, breathes massively.

The train is curving out of Fife, out along the gray steel curve of the Tay Bridge, high above the gray-green waves of the mile-wide river. Further out, the bridge's high girders are like a thronged pavement of friendly faces, one of the great familiars of his life, a badge of his place on the map, a badge of homecoming, of home. Beyond the high girders, the home curve, the long gentle downhill into Tay Bridge Station, and beyond all that, the heaped up mud-coloured walls and lums and spires and hills.

Dundee.

The one place in the world he could ever call home was in his eyes again. Never again, he tells himself, will I ever leave this place. They will never make me leave again.

At ease, soldier.

–18–

Tay Bridge Station. Stand down, soldier.

He stands down, then he just stands, motionless on the platform. The ground holds firm. He feels his feet beneath him. Nothing cloys or clings. Solid ground. He stands, feeling it. What now?

He scans the few early morning faces, recognises not one. His right eye will not focus.

A hesitant voice, behind him. Bob, it is saying. Bob.

He turns at the sound.

"Bob?"

He cannot find the sound.

"Bob Crumley. Is that you?"

Bob Crumley. That's him.

"Is that you?"

Margaret.

Not what he had hoped for. Not that he'd hoped at all, but if he had, not this…

He turns a face on her she barely recognises. He tries a smile, a salute.

"Lance Bombadier Crumley, reporting as requested."

He chokes back the next word that had sprung to his lips – "Sir".

Margaret can't choke back the words:

"Good heavens. You look as dead as Jean."

The dam breaks. His eyes fill and flood his face, tears touch the solid ground where he stands.

Nothing left to fight with.

Nothing left to fight.

Nothing left.

As dead as Jean.

Margaret tells him:

"We had to bury her on Christmas Eve."

No hug.

No welcome word.

No warmth.

Only an unconcealed repugnance for what the war to end wars had coughed up.

And no Jean to bury.

He asks amid the thud of carriage doors:

"The bairns?"

"With me. They'll be fine in time. You won't be able to help them now, not from the look of you."

Their silence fills with thudding buffers. The end of the line.

Then Margaret adds:

"I've been to your place. The neighbour, Agnes is it?, she'll put a fire on, give you your tea. You'll mind the way to the tram?"

Then she leaves him, backing away. Then she flees, running.

God but she was cahld.

The train shudders, moves off, steaming backwards. The sound suddenly puts in mind the wee pugs at Lochee station going backwards above the Railway Tavern. He moves off himself, a stood down soldier, takes the station steps at a slow march, the pace of a funeral, his small gesture to Jean. At the top, Union Street, and the smell of salt on the wind again. He turns up the street, one last march. Two hands on the ball, soldier.

He shoulders his kitbag, walks home, forgetting the way to the tram but not the homing instinct that draws him like a skylark to a nest in a field at the end of winter. Left right, left right, through the stirring streets, befriended by the ring of his own boots on his own pavements, by passing faces he recognises only as his own kind, voices he recognises only as those that speak his own language, the welcome of the mute and mud-coloured walls that built his place on the map.

Lochee at last, the High Street's curve, and where it straightens out, he pushes open the door of the close, hears his boots echo through the street-fronting houses, into the open courtyard beyond to where another three storey tenement block stands alone. He stops once, looks up, nods, walks on.

Aggie blah-baggie has been in, lit a fire, his lum reeks. She meets him at the door, throws her arms around him, puts her head against the bone-cage of his chest, lets him go. Her first words:

"Eh'll bring you in some tea."

He holds dear in his head for a moment the sound of that "Eh", as if it was Beethoven.

"Thanks Agnes. It's a sweet thing to see you."
She goes in to tell her man:
"Mr Walker's home. At least what's left of him is."
"He'll heal, Agnes. He'll heal."

– 19 –

The coal fire in the grate ablaze, but that house that he left clamorous with six bairns is as quiet as a purple dusk over France when the guns stopped. Quieter. There is no skylark.

Unlace the big boots. The last time.

Untie the tie. The last time.

He sits.

He stretches his six feet two inches of bone and little enough else across the hearth rug and grows still and warm. Agnes taps on the door and brings a pot of tea which she sets by the fire, and in the other hand a cup already poured, milk, two sugars.

"Eh'll get the pot back later. It's a spare ane onywey. Eh'll let masel oo'."

He nods. A raised hand waves his thanks. He has no words left. He closes his eyes. One eye will never re-awaken. He sleeps. And in the sleep of the un-dead, the dream takes hold of him for the first time.

Agnes taps back in again in the late afternoon, thinks maybe he's dead. The pot is where she left it. The cup is still half full, cold in one curved hand and wrist. She leans close and hears his breathing, creeps out.

The Goalie awakes late in the evening from the sound of a skylark singing over France. He looks around the room, the curtains pulled, a lamp on, the fire stoked. Agnes has been back. There is a fog in his right eye. He rubs it, but it does not clear.

−20−

Do you begin to see what has happened here? Do you see how the survival of one soldier through that war to end wars that finished more than eighty years ago goes on casting ripples? They touch my life. They touch yours too, for they are as much your inheritance as mine. This is your family album too.

If he had died in France he would have been twice a hero. The Goalie and the Soldier. A whole page in the *Courier*, eh? We would not be having this conversation, and there would be no family controversy to trouble me. But he came home alive, and dead on his feet, and too early for a hero's welcome and too late to bury his dead wife. He found his house emptied of his own bairns, and not enough of a mind left to raise a whimper about it.

But those bairns themselves – my father and uncles and aunts (and in time their wives and husbands who became ensnared in it all and complied with it all, wittingly or unwittingly) – they left no word of these things. How could they? They were bairns. My father was three when the Goalie went off to that war to end wars. Three! What would he have made of the ghost who came home a week after his mother had died? Nightmares?

No-one told them, then or later, either what he went through or the kind of man who came home. How could they ever have understood? Their father was shut away from them like a leper. I can almost understand it. There was no "post-traumatic stress", no "Gulf War Syndrome". The ones who came back were expected to get on with it. Some of them could not, and for a while at least, he was one of them. Instead of counsellors, there was Aggie blah-baggie, dispensing tea, and if she revelled out of his earshot in the gossip that must have clung to him as unhappily as a demob suit, her heart bled for him too, because he was one of her own, child of the same streets, and his troubles were her troubles. And the rest of it was up to him.

But you have to wonder why the bairns were *never* told, when they were older, when some kind of healing between father and bairns might have been achieved, and submerged love given the chance to resurface. It never happened.

No-one told them, so no-one told me. Instead the calumny was perpetuated and handed down. They told me what they *had* been told and never thought to challenge – that he was a waster, a lout, a drunk, devoid of any spark of humanity's saving graces, that he turned his back on his wife and children, cared only for his footballing hey-day when he was an icon, a hero among the men and women of his streets, cadging drinks on the strength of his past and careless of his family's plight. But a good goalie.

And how, at the end, he was so despised there was no-one to bury him and so he lay in a pauper's grave up the Hully.

You remember. My mother told us both that. You were there in the room, a few months before she died. It wasn't the first time I had heard her say it, but with you there, it was as if she was determined his infamy should live on, you having shown a bit of an aptitude for goalkeeping yourself.

She died believing these things, because her husband, my father, one of the Goalie's six bairns, told her. He told her because it was what he was told, and she died believing it because he died believing it, and they were both convinced enough to pass it on to their own son. Yet she never even met the man.

And you know what I think is at the bottom of it all?

Love.

Love runs deep, burns with rare passion in this family. I think of my mother's love for my father which did not falter once in the twenty years between his death and hers. She could have remarried, had the offer, but the hold of that love wouldn't let her.

I think of my father's love for his aunt, and hers for him. He was her favourite, I think, and when he died in his early sixties, she lost interest in life and died with him.

Such love blinds reason.

It permits no questions.

It believes utterly.

It lies to itself to protect itself and it believes its own lies.

And perhaps the greatest love of all of them was the one Margaret once felt for the Goalie. Does that surprise you? Think about it. The most damaging love because it was unrequited? And because he fell for her sister instead?

And because when Jean died and the war to end wars threw up the Goalie's shell on the shore of the Tay and Margaret was left to pick up the pieces of that love her sister had known, the love that spawned the six bairns fathered by the man whose bairns she had craved herself? Do you wonder that truth was a casualty of all this?

The Goalie went blind, as you know. You know because I told you. There are no pictures of an old blind man in the family album. Not one of my own family ever told me. Not once. Why not? In case I felt sympathy for the man they had spent a lifetime reviling? Unless, of course, they never knew.

Does that sound preposterous? Yet if I learned one thing for certain it is the preposterous nature of the Goalie's bairns' ignorance of their own father.

I know what you're thinking. If they knew so little, learned so little of the truth in all their lifetimes, how come I have learned so much in such a short time? How come I think I'm right and they're wrong – *so* wrong?

The answer is in that other family tradition which, forbye the goalkeeping, seems to be percolating down through my bloodline and yours, and goes back at least as far as the Goalie's eldest son who was a stalwart of Fleet Street. The journalist in me couldn't leave him alone. He was always there in the wings. Folk in these very streets were forever tapping me on the shoulder:

"Any relation to the Goalie?"

From the first teenage day I went looking for my first newspaper stories among them, he wouldn't leave me alone. He became mysterious, and in his way, glorious. An offbeat, spectral presence haunting the fringes of family memory like a barn owl going along the edge of a wood at dusk, somehow unsettling. And a name I realised I could drop in the company of strangers, knowing (eventually) that strangers who had known him outwith the confines of the family saw him quite differently.

Over the years, there grew the sense of a bond I can't define. I played football from birth almost. I played in goal, eventually. Strictly amateur, of course, but I loved it, and I felt something beyond the game itself standing between the goalposts in Lochee Park with the dark, benevolent crouch of the Hully throwing its winter shadows over frosted Saturdays. I felt at ease there, at home, in a way I have not done since in any other place. There was some kind of destiny's touch, some quiet bond.

I would hear a whistle and my throat would tighten. There was a free kick once, twenty yards out, driven high, heading for the left hand top corner. One step, a climbing dive, going for a fingertip over the bar and a voice in my head says:

"Two hands on the ball, son."

I catch it. I don't know how. Logic says it's beyond me. But I catch it and my team mates can't believe it. I hit the frosted ground with the ball clutched against my chest. I bounce back up and there is our centre-forward on halfway, on his own, with his hand raised, and I throw it from where I stand, my best throw follows my best save. He traps it, turns, runs half the length of the field and scores.

That was it. That was my cup final. My 1910. I don't even remember who we were playing or who won or what the score was. I remember the moment, the voice, the bond it forged. The voice didn't surprise me. It seemed the most natural thing, and I never heard it again. But I began to wonder about him more, to think about him more often. It grew slowly until I left the newspaper office to write my books and turned a writer's eye on the old ancestral homeland.

He cropped up. He would. He was part of the story, Dundee's story, Lochee's story, my story. And now your story. I wrote to my old paper asking for memoirs from the living. A few men and one woman came forward, old now but folk who knew him when they were young and the Goalie was old. One of them had been a footballing bairn in the street where he would sit on the windowsill. Their stories, and what they remembered their parents telling them, were so precious to me. They let in his humanity and my search for him began.

Perhaps that explains the voice and the save, eh? Perhaps I imagined the whole thing? Who cares? From his wherever, perhaps he saw in me a way into the family album?

At first, I set out to achieve a healing like a missionary. I would start with that pauper's grave, find it, and put up a stone. But I never did put up the stone because it was the work of a couple of days of simple research to prove that the pauper's grave story was someone's lie. He was cremated.

That is how deep the thing went. Look. Here's the death certificate. So what my father told my mother was a lie, and what my mother told me was a lie, but knowing the kind of people they were, I cannot believe they knew they were lying. My father saw no reason to challenge what he had been told and it was as simple as that. Except, of course, that there is nothing simple about it.

And far from dying in squalid disreputability (another piece of family propaganda), he was honoured by a crowd of hundreds including the whole Dundee team of the day. It was the work of five minutes more in the library's obituary books to uncover that. Five minutes, yet my father and mother never took that five minutes or ever thought to.

There had to be a reason. There *was* a reason.

It could only be that the source of all they were told was, in the eyes of the six bairns, so utterly trustworthy that it was beyond questioning, ever. There was only one such source. She was the woman who had brought them all up, gave them the lost love of their dead mother, sacrificed her own life in the process. The woman who could not muster a hug for the shell of the Goalie who came home from the war to end wars. The woman whose laugh froze to silence. The woman who stood in Lochee High Street laughing and locking eyes with the Goalie one bright day in 1904 when he barged into Jean and knocked her to the pavement. It can only have been her. It is the only explanation. She was the person my father held dearer than any other human alive; the woman he wrote to from the North African desert in 1941 with the words "to the best Auntie a soldier ever had".

It had to be her. It had to be Margaret.

-21-

He's about to apologise and help the lass up from the pavement when he hears the laugh. Sweet and contralto, and seductive on his ears. He straightens again and catches the eyes that laugh, the tossed dark hair, the tall, lithe, laughing dancer. He likes what he sees. So does she. They introduce themselves, eyes still locked. From somewhere below them:

"I'm terribly sorry for being breenged into by you. Please forgive me. Please excuse me while I get to my feet absolutely unaided. It is really no trouble at all."

And now the Goalie laughs. Dishevelled Jean with her doup on the pavey and her knee seeping blood onto her skirt and a few strands of her fair hair loose and fallen across her face, unfurls a smile of her own, wide-mouthed and round-faced and looking as if the sun had just risen on her. A bit pink.

He would tell her that often in the next few years, but for now he looks down, reaches two huge hands, snatches her up by the waist (ignoring her own outstretched hands), sets her on her feet, apologises with some style, asks her upstairs to clean up.

"Dinna think yer wife'd be affa pleased at that," she laughs.

"Wife? Nae wife. But the hoose is clean enough if that's what's bothering you. Eh could aye marry you of course, then you could go upstairs whenever you felt like it, and not just to clean up."

Confident, would you say?

She laughs again, and Margaret's laugh overlaps hers, so that he turns back to Margaret and adds:

"Or…Eh could marry you."

"And what makes you think either of us'd have you?" says Margaret.

"Oh, I'll have him," says Jean. There's a hat shop in the back of her head.

She laughs again and Margaret out-laughs her, and the Goalie smiles from one to the other and falls in love at first sight twice.

"We're only minutes from home," says Margaret, "and we can clean up fine there" and she steps off and Jean follows.

"Well you always know where you can bump into me," he says, and as he stares after them, his eye follows the lithe dancer more eagerly, but it's Jean who looks back over her shoulder, just once, and leaves a smile on the air behind her like a scent.

But unknown to him, he has just come between two arm-in-arm sisters, unlinked them forever, and hobnailed the dancer once and for all.

−22−

"Jess, can I ask you a favour?"

"Of course."

"You haven't heard it yet."

"Of course is still the answer."

"Ah Jess, if only…"

"If only what?"

"If only there weren't so many if onlys…"

"What the hell's that? Poetry? What is it you wanted to ask? Plain Scots this time, eh?"

"It's aboo' the speech."

"Well, you can't be lost for words. That's never happened."

"No, not lost, Jess, just…Eh'm no sure Eh've got the right ones."

"So you want me to read it?"

"Listen to it. It's just in meh heid."

"You've never memorised it?"

"Not so much memorised it as not written it down. Can't read withoo' meh glasses, and you ken how Eh hate wearin they glasses in public. They make me look ahld."

"And how would you know what they make you like. Anyway, you *are* ahld."

They both giggle at their own wee jokes. She thinks they are good together. He is old, she no more than youthfully middle-aged, but they both enjoy a few snatched minutes before opening time or after closing time, and just talk. The kind of talk that the cronies in parliamentary drinking session never permit. Quiet, compatible, intimate talk.

It was the intimacy he missed most, that kind of intimacy when the speaking mouths and the listening ears and (he remembers wistfully) the looking eyes are close enough to catch every carefully and carelessly placed nuance. Jessie envied Jean only that in the few years they had shared she would have enjoyed his eyes. It was that absence of intimacy, Jessie decided, that was why he'd asked her to marry him, out of the blue, December 12, 1929. The second eye was going by then, his city and his world darkening and confusing and unfocussing day by day. When he asked her, she didn't say yes or no or she'd need time to think about it, she just said:

"Why Bob?"

"Eh'm needin other eyes, Jess. Your eyes see more good in the world than any other eyes Eh've ever met. Eh'd like your eyes to look out for me."

She had put her hand on his and sat in silence for half an hour. Then she told him. She'd said yes to Willie, two days before. And then she told him that no-one had ever said anything more beautiful to her in her life, and he said he was not just losing his sight, he was losing his timing too, but that she'd be better off with Willie by far. Then she'd said:

"But never fear, Bob, I'll look out for you."

For that moment, that single moment in her life, she loved two men equally, but her decision was already made and she was grateful for that. They drank to each other. It was, she thought, the last time he saw the colour of her eyes with any clarity. Green eyes, she had, bonnie green eyes. And ever after they drank to each other in the quiet intimate moments their lives allowed them, and they never stopped wondering.

She looks at him now and wonders how different it would have been with him these twenty years, wonders if, as he aged and faded, she'd have sought consolation of a kind with Willie – or whoever – anyway, and finds she can't answer. Willie had kept her young and interested, in herself as well as him. The Goalie would probably have aged her quicker, but maybe she would have grown deeper too, in her mind. She would like her mind to have grown deeper.

And he considers her now and wonders how different it would have been with her, wonders if, as he aged and faded, she'd have sought consolation of a kind with Willie – or whoever – anyway. Maybe not, he thinks, for she's been loyal to Willie and would have been as loyal to him for all the differences in their ages. She'd have put colour into his life, which may not be the first thing you might think a blind man would latch on to, but he knew his life to be bare and hard-edged and she'd have coloured it and softened the edges, textured them with the particular kind of love she might have learned in time. She'd have brought him solace, consideration, warmth, humanity, kind words that

had nothing to do with who he was one day in 1910...
precious gifts of a woman's heart quite unknown to the
mak-wey-fur-the-Goalie cameraderie of those men who still
idolised him for his once-upon-a-times. She'd have let him
live in the present alongside the game that always lived on in
him, always would, not that it felt now as if there was much
time left. She'd have given him a reason for his tomorrows
while they still dawned, reasons to get up in the morning, to
go home in the evening, to lie down at night. Colour.

She puts a hand on his arm.

And touch. She'd have given him touch.

"Give us yer speech, Winston."

And humour.

She'd have given him humour to spar with and spark
off.

"Sure?"

"Sure."

So he stands, takes two paces back into the middle of
the empty bar room. She leans towards him across the bar
from the other side, admiring the stance, the bearing, the
poise.

And admiring glances.

She'd have given him admiring glances.

He begins:

–23–

"People of the city of Dundee…"

"Wait, wait. Are you not going to single out the Lord Provost and civic toffs for special mention at the start?"

"No."

"Why not?"

"Who's the guest of honour here, me or the Lord Provost?"

"You are."

"Right. First and last time in meh life. Besides, Eh can see no reason to mak special mentions. Especially the Lord Provost. Eh don't even know the man. He doesn't know me. They'll all be the same to me. And you've just given me an idea."

"No charge. What is it?"

"A new beginning. How about…

"People of the City of Dundee…you will forgive me if I make no reference to the more distinguished guests, as would be traditional. You all look the same to me."

She laughs.

And laughter.

She'd have given him laughter. His mind wanders off that way again. Jessie prompts him back.

"Is that it?"

His head shakes sadly. His demeanour slumps. He regrets asking her. He has no wish to be anyone's guest of honour. He has no wish to parade himself, old, slow, stiff and blind, the last survivor of the eleven, a relic. They will never let him forget. Never. One game of football, forty years before. Suddenly it seems pointless, shabby. He doesn't want to do it. He won't go.

"I won't do it, Jess."

"Stage fright?"

"No."

"You want to forget and they won't let you?"

And mind reading.

She would read his mind. Then she says:

"You don't want to forget, Bob, but you want the memory private. Sorry, Bob, but you're public property. How often have you sat here over the years and told as much of the world as cared to listen how football is ingrained in the soul of the Scottish working man? How it lifts him out of himself. How, because every single one of them has kicked a ball somewhere, sometime, even if it's only in the street, they can identify with their heroes, and think: 'that could have been me'. Well it *was* you, Bob. You are one of the ones who gave them their dreams, who let them rise above themselves. You won the Scottish Cup. You. For Dundee. You brought it home. The Scottish Cup. What could be better than that?"

He says it softly:

"Playing for Scotland."

She snaps back:

"No. Not for these people. For you, maybe, but not for them! Not for their dreams, not for their city and their streets and the way they talk and the smell of the lums and the sea and all the other things that make this place what it is that's different fae every other place on earth. For them, it was winning the Cup, bringing it back, parading it in the streets, passing round bottles of whisky in the streets, whisky many of them couldn't afford and couldn't afford to be without. And the thing about it is, Bob, my dear…"

My dear.

She would say 'My dear' to him. The way she sometimes said it to Willie when she thought no-one could hear. He'd never thought about that before.

"And the thing about it is, Bob, my dear, that it only ever happened once. That's what makes it special. That's what makes it what it is, and in their eyes, it's what makes you what they think you are. It may have been forty years ago, and you may be sick to your bones of having it cast up day after day, but you did it, you're the only one who did it, and until it gets done again, you're still the only one. You and the other ten and they're all dead. You're the single focus left for all their dreams. The dreams, as you told us one night not that long ago, you dreamed yourself when you were seven, and never stopped dreaming them until they came true. Because you gave everything for the dream and they gave nothing. But they love you for living their dream. And that's what the point of all this is. And that's why you're the Guest of Honour."

And reassurance.

She'd have given him reassurance. He laughs.

"Jess. Will you marry me?"

"I'll have to ask Willie."

"He won't mind. It won't be for long."

She fancies a shadow crossing his face, a troubling thing.

"What makes you say that?"

"The dream."

"What, the one I was just talking about, or *the* dream?"

"*The* dream."

"What about it?"

"Nae skehlark."

"Don't follow."

"Eh dreamed it last night. There was nae skehlark."

"It's a dream, Bob."

"Last night, Jess, Eh died in the dream."

"So what? You woke up."

He frowns. He did. He woke up. When he died in the dream, felt the bayonet go deep between his ribs and died, he dragged himself awake and lay there at three in the morning and knew it for a sign. He's dying.

"Eh'm dying," he convinces himself aloud. Then Jessie says, simple as you like, "so what...you woke up".

–24–

"You know who'd be proud of you if you stand up and do it?" Jessie asks him.

"Billy Steele?"

He namedrops Dundee's current football icon, not a goalie but a good player for all that.

"No. Jean."

He frowns again. Jean…it's been so long. Sometimes he can't recall the sound of her voice. More than thirty years since she died, add the war years he didn't see her. She would have been 66. He remembers only a woman not yet 30.

He nods at Jessie. Jean loved to dress. Loved an occasion, turned the bairns out well whenever the occasion arose for all that he drank as much as he gave her. Then, it was expected, you see. You played the game for 90 minutes at a time, but you played the Goalie, the icon, 24 hours a day. Jessie's right – he is public property.

He wonders silently, should he do it for Jean?

No.

This is nothing to do with Jean. It's his turmoil, not hers. Jean was like a watershed that divided his life. When she died and Margaret took in the bairns and the war to end wars had finished with him, he crossed that watershed, or at least he stumbled among its bogs and tussocks and boulderfields. But the crossing – in time, when he could put one foot in front of another again and think straight – the crossing was irrevocable.

"Do you ever think of her?" Jessie, easing him back to the here and now.

"Not much. Not now. She bore the bairns I hardly knew and they bore the grandchildren I never knew. She's still 30 years old, I'm 75. What could I think of her that would help either her or me? But you're right, she would have loved the show."

"But it's not her show, right?"

Yes, and mind-reading. She would read his mind.

Perhaps he remembered the 17-year-old Jean best, the one he bumped into, better than the one who died on him, if only because of the guilt that swamped him because he survived the war to end wars in France and she died at home in Dundee. And maybe the guilt was why he stopped thinking of her much. But sometimes he did remember when life was good, when Margaret with the looks and the dancer's legs and the dark hair would lead him on so far and then be cool, always looking to control his celebrity and tame it.

And Jean would somehow start to make a habit of turning up wherever he happened to be, and whenever he asked her she was warm and willing and just as often she was warm and willing without being asked, and he chose warm and willing. She was 19 when they married, he was 27. He was at the peak of his powers and for five more years his fame among the mud-coloured streets just grew and Jean had her Prince Charming, and it was better than being married to a weaver or a shopkeeper, much as she still turned over the hat shop in her mind.

You could not say he was the most devoted of fathers, nor husbands, and his fame legislated against both, but they loved well, the two of them, and put six healthy bairns on the streets of Lochee. She gave them the nest. He gave them the wings.

Jessie looks at him with love of a kind, that aspect of love Wille didn't need from her. Willie had her heart and her body and her loyalty. She gave the Goalie her eyes, to look out for him. That kind of love.

"What about Margaret?"

"What about her?"

"Ever see her?"

She could use that "see" the way he did.

"Eh cross the street if Eh see her coming."

He reverses thirty years back through his life, a rewinding spool until he hits the gray years of 1919 and 1920. That Lochee then saw him through. Through the gray years, when his war-warped mind and his blinded eye and his embittered heart drank their way through sundry oblivions. Lochee remembered who he was, that he was one of them, that he had climbed out of the streets by his football studs but never left them, that he lived their dreams for them, and they saw to it that he came through. Through the drinking, the brawling, the delirious havering, the war madness. They soothed his brow and and put him to bed and woke him up and made him breakfast and made him tea, and got him a job as a corporation messenger, and when it was all done and settled into nothing more tormenting than the ritual of the dream, Margaret came to tell him that his bairns were her bairns, that if he ever wanted to see them again, he'd to marry her, which is what he should have done in the first place, she said, instead of that slut of a sister of hers. Then he hit her. Just once, and it stung him out of his madness forever. Double Ecky's intervention kept him out of court and probably jail, but by then Margaret had seen to it that there was not a magistrate in Dundee who would let him lay a finger on his own bairns.

So they grew up hating him and Margaret kept the bairns she felt should have been hers anyway, though they were fruit of her sister's womb and she never forgave her dead sister or the man she lay with to father them. Margaret knew no man after that and died a spinster adored by the bairns who had long since ceased to know their father and could scarcely remember their mother at all.

The Goalie grew quiet and fatalistic, settled for his lot, for the curving embrace of Lochee High Street and the wider, sea-going city beyond, and the daily company of the folk who got him through.

"Folk like you, Jess, folk like you," he tells her and the backwards film in his head stops and runs forward again and stops at April 19, 1950.

"Jean would have loved the show. But this has nothing to do with Jean. It's about me and what's left of my life. I won't do it. I won't need the speech. I won't need you to listen. But thanks for offering. Sorry, lass."

"You must never apologise to me, Bob, for being who you are and what you are. There is not a man and woman in this street who doesn't love you in their own ways for who or what you are. Remember that. Forget that and you're done for. Remember it and you'll outlive us all."

She pours him a drink, first of the day.

"Was it a good speech?"

"Good enough."

– 25 –

People of the City of Dundee. You will forgive me if I make no reference to the more, um, distinguished guests. You all look the same to me.

You have made me your Guest of Honour.

Thank you.

What took you so long?

Guest of Honour. I wasn't sure what was involved, so I consulted Lochee's cleverest man, Ecky Smellie. It's not that he's particularly clever, just that he's the only man in Lochee with a dictionary. You and I both know that a dictionary is as much use to a blind man as a football team is without a Goalie, which is worse than useless. But Ecky does crosswords, which means he can read, and sometimes a blind man has to get by with other people's een.

So I got him to turn up "honour" and asked him to read. It's the "Oxford", mind, not just any old dictionary.

So he thumbs through the pages, scratching his head because I won't tell him why I want to know, and he reads aloud the entry under "honour":

"Respect, esteem, reverence, reputation, glory, distinction, mark of…"

OK, stop, never mind the mark of bit…just up to distinction. Again.

So he reads again, and I listen, hearing it differently from the way he's saying it. I start to hear it, to see it, like this:

Respect

Esteem   Reverence

Reputation   Glory   Distinction

Respect for the Goalie. That's good. As it should be.

Esteem at right back, Reverence at left back, good qualities dependable qualities, what you need in full backs.

Reputation, Glory and Distinction. What a half-back line!

You build a good football team from the back, not from the front. You build with respect, for your game and for your team-mates, and for your opponents. Because football is a game. And the game is nothing at all without the other side. But it is a special kind of game, one ingrained in the soul of the Scottish working class man (and in the working class woman although she is not always willing to show it), and the stuff of his dreams. I have been lucky. I have lived other people's dreams. And because I was a part – one eleventh part – of a team that won a game forty years ago today, you honour me. I hardly think it is appropriate.

If you were to show me respect you would leave me in peace. I am an old man with my memories. Few enough of them have anything to do with football, and were it not for the fact that you, the people of Dundee, have sustained me in so many ways since I stopped playing football and my life grew empty for too many years, I would long since have been in the same place as the other ten players who shared the Scottish Cup with me.

So if you would truly do me the honour, and if you would truly confer its meanings on me – respect, esteem, reverence, reputation, glory, distinction – then do this with me. Please stand up.

Now, be silent for two minutes. Pay respect to the others. And as you hear the names, don't see them like words on a page, see them as I see them, on a cloth of green and arranged like this:

	2 *Neil*		3 *McEwan*	
4 *Lee*		5 *Dainty*		6 *Comrie*
7 *Bellamy*	8 *Langlands*	9 *Hunter*	10 *McFarlane*	11 *Fraser*

Thank you.
Please sit down.

As you have seen fit not to leave me in peace, and I have seen fit to return the compliment and not leave you in peace either, we must all get through these few minutes as best we can. As you can appreciate, there is not much call for a goalie thirty-eight years retired to make speeches, and never let what goes on in the Railway Tavern be confused wi speech.

I am, as you know, blind. A blind man, or a blind woman, works harder with what's left. For example, you see with your mind. And that can deepen you because you see and think with the same thing. So you think deeper and you see deeper. Instead of just looking at things you look inside things.

And as being blind goes, I'm lucky. I wasn't always blind. And when I went blind, I went blind slowly. I could adjust. I could, you might say, see it coming. So I know what things look like. I know what my own city looks like, and I happen to think it's a beautiful place. I don't mean it possesses the skin-deep beauty that a pair of good eyes might like to look on. No-one would claim that for this city. What I mean is the deep beauty that a mind's eye sees. You would all revere your birthplace a lot more and look after it a lot better, if you had to walk around for a week with your eyes shut.

The other thing you can do is apply the colour you want. From where I stand, the Lord Provost is wearing a scarlet jacket, yellow breeks and a Royal Stewart tartan shirt. You may think he's wearing black and white, but then you're all wearing emerald green and silver!

There are better things to do with colour than make jokes with it though. I only ever see a blue sea. And when I take a slow stroll up the Cooie Roadie to the Hully, I see autumn trees. So I have taken your city and mine, rubbed out all the skin-deep eyesores and perfected the rest. It is such a beautiful place you all live in. Never forget it. And don't let the fact that you have eyes to look at it fool you.

I never much wanted to be any place but here. Odd days up in the hills, odd days down at the sea, odd days across the Tay on the Fifies. But mostly, just here. The streets and the folk in them. The Law Hill and the Hully. The Tay. I couldn't desire more.

I could have been a tailor, you know, learned the trade. Football saved me from it. Gave me the glorious years of my life. And because I played football when I did, and had the luck to be part of a very good team, and because I went blind…when I fell flat on my arse (and I did, really fell, really flat) after that "War to end Wars", I was saved and my life was saved, and it made me deeper and richer. Not money richer, mind, just richer.

If I had been a tailor, not a footballer, I'd probably not have been a soldier, not fought, not gone blind, not fallen flat, not done much of anything. But I played. I was good. I fought. I fell. I went blind. And when I started to get up again, I began to learn the worth of life.

The people who taught me were not teachers, not professors or scientists or geniuses. They were weavers, blacksmiths, cleaners, publicans, shopkeepers, tram drivers, a stationmaster, a policeman, coalies, milkies, scrappies, scaffies. Folk who gave me the time of day, every day I asked for it and every day I didn't. They picked me up when I fell over. And if I had begun this speech with a tribute to the Lord Provost and the other civic dignitaries, it would have been a betrayal of the folk who picked me up.

However long I live – and it canna be lang now – I will never betray them. They are my life and without them you would have had no Guest of Honour.

Thank you.

-26-

Do you see the old blind man across the street, sitting alone on a low windowsill with his feet on the pavement, slightly bent at the waist, stiff as a rusted hinge? That's him. The Goalie. They made a cigarette card of him, you know. An icon in his day.

Do you see what he's doing now? Look how only his head moves. See? He's watching the bairns playing football in the street. He can do that. He went blind gradually and his ears became his eyes. See! He knows every move and who makes it. Their voices and their sounds have become their faces. Do you see how he turns his face away from where the ball is? Turns his ear towards it? Hear how the noise always accompanies the ball.

Do you know what he should be doing today? It's the 20th of April, 1950. Forty years to the day. He's to be guest of honour of the Lord Provost at a special dinner. He's the last of the cup-winning team alive. A walking relic. He won't go.

He won't make the speech he prepared. He won't be their guest. He knew all along, knew he had a prior engagement. He told the Lord Provost's office almost as soon as the invitation arrived, thanks but no thanks, and then, he kind of flirted with the idea in his mind, made up the speech, wondered what Jessie would make of it. A last, foolish attempt to impress her maybe, and maybe something more, something much more than that. But, you see, there's a football match at Dens tonight, in the light early evening, a friendly, a charity game, but still a football match. And every football match at Dens Park he goes along and stands with a little group of men on the terraces just by the half way line.

– 27 –

They wouldn't tell you about this. They didn't tell me either. I imagine it was one more thing they didn't know about him. Do you notice anything about the men he's standing with? They're all blind.

He has a box beside the wall. He stands on it just before kick-off, so that he's head and shoulder above the others. Then…well, listen. Listen to him. Do you hear what he's doing? He's commentating. He knows the game so well, you see, from within.

He knows the ground so well, too, the pitch. He knows how the game sounds when it's in a particular part of the pitch. He knows the voices of the Dundee players, knows the sound of a short pass or a long punt, a bounce or a header. And of course he reads the voice of the crowd too. All this he takes in and turns it into commentary for the other blind lads, the blind leading the blind. He misses nothing. He can answer their questions.

You notice too that the lads behind the group aren't blind at all. But they like to listen. They all know who he is, of course, know who he was, know he lived their dreams for them, and they go and stand behind him and lend him their ears. And if he happens to struggle now and again with a name they help him out. That is why he won't be the Lord Provost's Guest of Honour.

What he does not know is that there is a conspiracy afoot. When the Lord Provost found out why the invitation was declined, he decided to call a couple of friends on the Dundee board. You know how it is among the ruling classes of a city like this. Two or three phone calls can fix anything. He nobbled the board. The board nobbled the players. The players nobbled the blind lads. And at full time, the blind lads will nobble the Goalie.

"Right lads, see you on Saturday." The Goalie prepares to take his leave.

"No so fast, Goalie," says one of the blind lads. "Yer wanted out on the pitch."

"On the pitch. Na, na, Geordie, they haven't wanted me on the pitch for 38 years."

The tannoy confirms it.

"Mr Robert Crumley to the centre circle, please. Robert Crumley. The Goalie."

And they manhandle him over the low wall onto the pitch, the other blind lads, a couple of policemen with eyes. Suddenly he's on the pitch and the other blind lads are beside him, laughing, thumping his shoulders, while he shakes his head.

The tannoy tells everyone:

"Forty years ago today…"

The penny drops. The mountain has come to Mohammed. The Lord Provost has brought the show to him, brought it to *his* place, *his* theatre. That's different. He'll walk *this* stage.

He stops them, strings the blind lads out in a line, fifteen of them, stands in the middle of the line, puts an arm round the shoulders of the lads on each side, tells them all to do likewise, and then, "out the hellish legion sallied". Out in the centre circle he stops them again and they take a bow, like the Tiller Girls. A bit like the Tiller Girls. Then the other lads unlink and step back, and the crowd acclaims him, their love for him, for who he is, for who he was, for what he's done since, for living their dreams for them.

The blind lads begin to chant.

"Goa-lie! Goa-lie! Goa-lie!"

The crowd picks it up and it grows. It runs round the ground as it grows. He hears it again, the gray music. The grateful opened throats, that noise that runs round the ground like a fire before a wind. That music.

That music won the Scottish Cup and brought it home to Dundee forty years ago to the day.

The Lord Provost steps forward, shakes the Goalie's hand, says a few appropriate words no-one can remember into a microphone, presents a plaque in honour of the occasion, and in his ear, whispers:

"Nae bugger stands up the Lord Provost of the City and Royal Burgh of Dundee."

Then he steps back and says into the microphone:

"Would we all like to hear a few words from the Goalie?"

The crowd takes five unbroken minutes to deliver its answer.

"Goa-lie! Goa-lie! Goa-lie!"

On and on, thousands of opened throats. That music. He takes the microphone. Two hands on the ball.

"People of the City of Dundee…"

"Goa-lie! Goa-lie! Goa-lie!"

They roar it again.

"You will forgive me if I make no reference to the more, um, distinguished guests. You all look the same to me…"

They roar. That music. Wonderful music. Crazy as a loon. Sad as a gipsy serenading the moon.

−28−

He wakes up one morning soon after that night and realises out loud:

"Nae dream…"

He goes down to the Railway Tavern before morning opening and tells Jess:

"Nae dream."

"So. Is that unusual?"

"The last ten years, every night. That dream. Sometimes the days too."

"What? When you're awake?"

"Aye, sometimes, when the heid's tired, it just creeps in."

"Well, you still woke up."

"I did. But this is the run-in, Jess. I'll give it six months."

"Well I'll give it six years. Ten bob note."

"You'll lose."

"Well, even if I do, you'll be in no position to collect."

"Ten bob note against a round on the house to drink to my improving health in the afterlife."

"Done."

They spit on their right palms, then rub them together, his huge hand, hard and jagged with the humps of rearranged bones, the goalie's traditional legacy, hers small and firm, long fingered. But the dream has done with him. His war is finally over. He has made his peace. It will give him six months.

−29−

The last autumn, he was still peching up the beloved hillside, up out of the streets to where he could sense his city curve away below him to the Tay. The river widened eastward to the sea, and the sea was always blue, a mile-wide miracle as it passed Dundee, wider than anything he could think of after it passed Broughty Ferry's wave-butting castle. He loved the river without thinking why. It was what made where he lived better than where anyone else lived, coming up the hill out of the streets until you could see the river. That and the hill itself, the Balgay Hill, the Hully, his very own place on the map of the world. Here where a boy with a burst nose announced to the world he was the goalie and discovered skylarks all in the same day. He loved it forever.

He felt tired and sat down.

He felt the sun on his face and raised his sightlessness to it. Autumn sun was always the sweetest.

He felt a pain in his left hand, where the ball had clung on to his curved palm, that palm that had curved round it despite himself. What did he do that for?

It was the last thing he ever felt. They found him sitting there, his head forward over his knees. Full time. Final score: Life 0 Death 11.

– 30 –

So that's your great-grandfather for you. Or at least it's my idea of him. Either way, it's nearer the truth than his own family was ever prepared to accept.

How's your glass? I'm thirsty. I talk too much.

But I don't like injustice. And I have found injustice among members of the same family as unforgiveable as it is bewildering. A whole generation of children was lied to and deluded about their own father because of a spinster's jealous grief, and maybe because of a war that wrecked his iconic former self. He *was* an icon in his way.

No child is ever better off by being denied such an elemental part of life as a truthful awareness of a compassionate man. I think he was a compassionate man...watching the bairns from the windowsill, commentating for the blind lads up at Dens Park.

No, he was not a flawless man. Which of us is, eh? But shouldn't a father be judged by his own children on the basis of what they know of him from their own contact with him, not from what they are told about him by others bearing grievances? It is in that way, for example, that I judged my own father, and you have to judge me. But my father was denied that right. He bore that immeasurable loss to his grave.

Make a better judgment than that, won't you? A truer judgment. That's what I ask of you. It's not much.

I told you I have a new family album for you. Here it is. I couldn't fill its pages with those snapshots of the Goalie's life I have just shown you, because, as I said a few hours ago now (I had no intention of keeping you so long, I'm sorry), they are pictures that were never taken or were lost, the moments not recorded or the record of them destroyed.

So what kind of family album can I offer you? Open it.

That's the cigarette card they made of him on the first page.

No, there's no point in turning the pages. That's all there is.

You see, there are no other pictures of him. All anyone took of his life, or all anyone kept, were football team pictures. Even the cigarete card is taken from a team group, the head and shoulders isolated and cut out from the rest. No childhood, no youth, no middle age, no old age. Just the few glorious years of his prime rendered static and arm-folded.

But the point is this. He was never in a family album before. He is now. Fill it. Fill it with all the generations you can. Fill it with your own family. For his sake.

Fill it for your own sake, and for the sake of all those generations who come after you and who will be spared the lies and the jealousies and who will turn the pages and simply be glad that he is there.

And yes, I declare my own interest. Fill it for my sake. If you have any love for your own father, fill it with all of us. He's our root, yours as well as mine. And he's no black sheep, he's just family.

And he's loved. He died, never knowing I existed. But I love the idea of him.

– 31 –

Skylark, have you anything to say to me?
Won't you tell me where my love can be?
Is there a meadow in the mist
Where someone's waiting to be kissed?
Skylark, have you seen a valley green with spring
Where my heart can go a-journeying,
Over the shadows and the rain
To a blossom-covered lane?

And in your lonely flight
Haven't you heard the music of the night?
Wonderful music,
Faint as a will o' the wisp,
Crazy as a loon,
Sad as a gipsy serenading the moon?

Oh skylark, I don't know if you can find these things,
But my heart is riding on your wings,
So if you see them anywhere,
Won't you lead me there?